# damned if i do

# damned if i do

STORIES

◆

*Percival Everett*

Graywolf Press

Publication of this volume is made possible in part by a grant provided by the Minnesota State Arts Board, through an appropriation by the Minnesota State Legislature; a grant from the Wells Fargo Foundation Minnesota; and a grant from the National Endowment for the Arts, which believes that a great nation deserves great art. Significant support has also been provided by the Bush Foundation; Target, Marshall Field's and Mervyn's with support from the Target Foundation; the McKnight Foundation; and other generous contributions from foundations, corporations, and individuals. To these organizations and individuals we offer our heartfelt thanks.

MINNESOTA
STATE ARTS BOARD

NATIONAL
ENDOWMENT
FOR THE ARTS

Published by Graywolf Press
212 Third Avenue North, Suite 485
Minneapolis, Minnesota 55401
All rights reserved.

www.graywolfpress.org

Published in the United States of America

ISBN 978-1-55597-411-4

8    10    12    13    11    9    7

Library of Congress Control Number: 2004104191

Cover design: VetoDesignUSA.com

Cover photographs: Digital Vision

# Acknowledgments

Grateful acknowledgment is made to the editors of the following publications in which these stories have appeared: *Callaloo, Fiction International, Idaho Review, New York Stories, Story,* and *Triquarterly.*

"Age Would Be That Does" also appeared in *Calling the Wind: Twentieth-Century African American Fiction,* ed. Clarence Major (New York: HarperCollins, 1993).

"Randall Randall" appeared in *Ancestral House: The Black Short Story in the Americas and Europe,* ed. Charles H. Rowell (New York: Westview Press, Perseus Books Group, 1995).

"The Appropriation of Cultures" also appeared in *The Pushcart Prize XXII,* ed. Bill Henderson with the Pushcart Prize editors, 1998.

*For Gene and George Rochberg*

# Contents

# damned if i do

◆

# The Fix

◆

Douglas Langley owned a little sandwich shop at the intersection of Fourteenth and T streets in the District. Beside his shop was a seldom-used alley and above his shop lived a man by the name of Sherman Olney, whom Douglas had seen beaten to near extinction one night by a couple of silky-looking men who seemed to know Sherman and wanted something in particular from him. Douglas had been drawn outside from cleaning up the storeroom by a rhythmic thumping sound, like someone dropping a telephone book onto a table over and over. He stepped out into the November chill and discovered that the sound was actually that of the larger man's fists finding again and again the belly of Sherman Olney, who was being kept on his feet by the second assailant. Douglas ran back inside and grabbed the pistol he kept in the rolltop desk in his business office. He returned to the scene with the powerful flashlight his son had given him and shone the light into the faces of the two villains.

The men were not overly impressed by the light, the bigger one saying, "Hey, man, you better get that light out of my face!"

They did however show proper respect for the discharging of the .32 by running away. Sherman Olney crumpled to the ground, moaning and clutching at his middle, saying he didn't have it anymore.

"Are you all right?" Douglas asked, realizing how stupid the question was before it was fully out.

But Sherman's response was equally insipid as he said, "Yes."

"Come, let's get you inside." Douglas helped the man to his feet and into the shop. He locked the glass door behind them, then took Sherman over to the counter and helped him onto a stool.

"Thanks," Sherman said.

"You want me to call the cops?" Douglas asked.

Sherman Olney shook his head. "They're long gone by now."

"I'll make you a sandwich," Douglas said as he stepped behind the counter.

"Really, that's not necessary."

"You'll like it. I don't know first aid, but I can make a sandwich." Douglas made the man a pastrami and Muenster on rye sandwich and poured him a glass of barely cold milk, then took him to sit in one of the three booths in the shop. Douglas sat across the table from the man, watched him take a bite of the sandwich.

"What did they want?" Douglas put to him.

"To hurt me," Sherman said, his mouth working on the tough bread. He picked a seed from his teeth and put it on his plate. "They wanted to hurt me."

"My name is Douglas Langley."

"Sherman Olney."

"What were they after, Sherman?" Douglas asked, but he didn't get an answer.

As they sat there, the quiet of the room was disturbed by the loud refrigerator motor kicking on. Douglas felt the vibration of it through the soles of his shoes.

"Your compressor is a little shot," Sherman said.

Douglas looked at him, not knowing what he was talking about.

"Your fridge. The compressor is bad."

"Oh, yes," Douglas said. "It's loud."

"I can fix it."

Douglas just looked at him.

"You want me to fix it?"

Douglas didn't know what to say. Certainly he wanted the machine fixed, but what if this man just liked to take things apart? What if he made it worse? Douglas imagined the kitchen floor strewn with refrigerator parts. But he said, "Sure."

With that, Sherman got up and walked back into the kitchen, Douglas on his heels. The skinny man removed the plate from the bottom of the big and embarrassingly old machine and looked around. "Do you have any chewing gum?" Sherman asked.

As it turned out, Douglas had, in his pocket, the last stick of a pack of Juicy Fruit, which he promptly handed over. Sherman unwrapped the stick, folded it into his mouth, then lay there on the floor chewing.

"What are you doing?" Douglas asked.

Sherman paused him with a finger, then, as if feeling the texture of the gum with his tongue, he took it from his mouth and stuck it into the workings of the refrigerator. And just like that the machine ran with a quiet steady hum, just like it had when it was new.

"How'd you do that?" Douglas asked.

Sherman, now on his feet, shrugged.

"Thank you, this is terrific. All you used was chewing gum. Can you fix other things?"

Sherman nodded.

"What are you? Are you a repairman or an electrician?" Douglas asked.

"I can fix things."

"Would you like another sandwich?"

Sherman shook his head again and said. "I should be going. Thanks for the food and all your help."

"Those men might be waiting for you," Douglas said. He suddenly remembered his pistol. He could feel the weight of it in his pocket. "Just sit in here awhile." Douglas felt a great deal of sympathy for the underfed man who had just repaired his refrigerator. "Where do you live? I could drive you."

"Actually, I don't have a place to live." Sherman stared down at the floor.

"Come over here." Douglas led the man to the big metal sink across the kitchen. He turned the ancient lever and the pipes started with a thin whistle and then screeched as the water came out. "Tell me, can you fix that?"

"Do you want me to?"

"Yes." Douglas turned off the water.

"Do you have a wrench?"

Douglas stepped away and into his business office,

where he dug his way through a pile of sweaters and newspapers until he found a twelve-inch crescent wrench and a pipe wrench. He took them back to Sherman. "Will these do?"

"Yes." Sherman took the wrench and got down under the sink.

Douglas bent low to try and see what the man was doing, but before he could figure anything out, Sherman was getting up.

"There you go," Sherman said.

Incredulous, Douglas reached over to the faucet and turned on the water. The water came out smoothly and quietly. He turned it off, then tried it again. "You did it."

"It's nothing. An easy repair."

"You know, I could really use somebody like you around here," Douglas said. "Do you need a job? I mean, do you want a job? I can't pay much. Just minimum wage, but I can let you stay in the apartment upstairs. Actually, it's just a room. Are you interested?"

"You don't even know me," Sherman said.

Douglas stopped. Of course the man was right. He didn't know anything about him. But he had a strong feeling that Sherman Olney was an honest man. An honest man who could fix things. "You're right," Douglas admitted. "But I'm a good judge of character."

"I don't know," Sherman said.

"You said you don't have a place to go. You can live here and work until you find another place or another job." Douglas was unsure why he was pleading so with the stranger and, in fact, had a terribly uneasy feeling about the whole business, but, for some reason, he really wanted him to stay.

"Okay," Sherman said.

Douglas took the man up the back stairs and showed him the little room. The single bulb hung from a cord in the middle of the ceiling and its dim light revealed the single bed made up with a yellow chenille spread. Douglas had taken many naps there.

'This is it," Douglas said.

"It's perfect." Sherman stepped fully into the room and looked around.

"The bathroom is down the hall. There's a narrow shower stall in it."

"I'm sure I'll be comfortable."

"There's food downstairs. Help yourself."

"Thank you."

Douglas stood in awkward silence for a while wondering what else there was to say. Then he said, "Well, I guess I should go on home to my wife."

"And I should get some sleep."

Douglas nodded and left the shop.

◆

Douglas's wife said, "Are you crazy?"

Douglas sat at the kitchen table and held his face in his hands. He could smell the ham, salami, turkey, Muenster, cheddar, and Swiss from his day's work. He peeked through his fingers and watched his short, plump wife reach over and turn down the volume of the television on the counter. The muted mouths of the news anchors were still moving.

"I asked you a question," she said.

"It sounded more like an assertion." He looked at her eyes, which were narrowed and burning into him. "He's a fine fellow. Just a little down on his luck, Sheila."

Sheila laughed, then stopped cold. "And he's in the shop all alone." She shook her head, her lips tightening across her teeth. "You have lost your mind. Now, you go right back down there and you get rid of that guy."

"I don't feel like driving," Douglas said.

"I'll drive you."

He sighed. Sheila was obviously right. Even he hadn't understood his impulse to offer the man a job and invite him to use the room above the shop. So, he would let her drive him back down there and he'd tell Sherman Olney he'd have to go.

They got into the old, forest green Buick LeSabre, Sheila behind the wheel and Douglas sunk down into the passenger seat that Sheila's concentrated weight had through the years mashed so flat. He usually hated when she drove, but especially right at that moment, as she was angry and with a mission. She took their corner at Underwood on two wheels and sped through the city and moderately heavy traffic back toward the shop.

"You really should slow down," Douglas said. He watched a man in a blue suit toss his briefcase between two parked cars and dive after it out of the way.

"You're one to give advice. You? An old fool who

takes in a stray human being and leaves him alone in your place of business is giving advice? He's probably cleaned us out already."

Douglas considered the situation and felt incredibly stupid. He could not, in fact, assure Sheila that she was wrong. Sherman might be halfway to Philadelphia with twelve pounds of Genoa salami. For all he knew Sherman Olney had turned on the gas of the oven, grilled his dinner, and blown the restaurant to smithereens. He rolled down his window just a crack and listened for sirens.

"If anything bad has happened, I'm having you committed," Sheila said. She let out a brief scream and rattled the steering wheel. "Then I'll sell what little we have left and spend the rest of my life in Bermuda. That's what I'll do."

When Sheila made marks on the street braking to a stop, the store was still there and not ablaze. All the lights were off and the only people on the street were a couple of hookers on the far corner. Douglas unlocked and opened the front door of the shop, then followed Sheila inside. They walked past the tables and counter and into the kitchen where Douglas switched on the bright overhead lights. The fluorescent tubes flickered, then filled the place with a steady buzz.

"Go check the safe," Sheila said.

"There was no money in it," Douglas said. "There never is." She knew that. He had taken the money home and was going to drop it at the bank on his way to work the next day. He always did that.

"Check it anyway."

He walked into his business office and switched on the standing lamp by the door. He looked across the room to see that the safe was still closed and that the stack of newspapers was still in front of it. "Hasn't been touched," he said.

"What's his name?" Sheila asked.

"Sherman."

"Sherman!" she called up the stairs. "Sherman!"

In short order, Sherman came walking down the stairs in his trousers and sleeveless undershirt. He was rubbing his eyes, trying to adjust to the bright light.

"Sherman," Douglas said, "it's me, Douglas."

"Douglas? What are you doing back?" He stood in front of them in his stocking feet. "By the way, I fixed the toilet and also that funny massager thing."

"You mean, my foot massager?" Sheila asked.

"If you say so."

"I told you, Sherman can fix things," Douglas said to Sheila. "That's why I hired him." Sheila had purchased the foot massager from a fancy store in Georgetown. On the days when she worked in the shop she used to disappear every couple of hours for about fifteen minutes and then return happy and refreshed. She would be upstairs in the bathroom, sitting on the closed toilet with her feet stationed on her machine. Then the thing stopped working. Sheila loved that machine.

"The man at the store said my foot massager couldn't be repaired," Sheila said.

Sherman shrugged. "Well, it works now."

"I'll be right back," Sheila said and she walked away from the men and up the stairs.

Sherman watched her, then turned to Douglas. "Why did you come back?"

"Well, you see, Sheila doesn't think it's a good idea that you stay here. You know, alone and everything. Since we don't know you or anything about you." Douglas blew out a long slow breath. "I'm really sorry."

Upstairs, Sheila screamed, then came running back to the top of the stairs. "It works! It works! He did fix it." She came down, smiling at Sherman. "Thank you so much."

"You're welcome," Sherman said.

"I was just telling Sherman that we're sorry but he's going to have to leave."

"Don't be silly," Sheila said.

Douglas stared at her and rubbed a hand over his face. He gave Sheila a baffled look.

"No, no, it's certainly all right if Sherman sleeps here. And tomorrow, he can get to work." She grabbed Sherman's arm and turned him toward the stairs. "Now, you get on back up there and get some rest."

Sherman said nothing, but followed her directions. Douglas and Sheila watched him disappear upstairs.

Douglas looked at his wife. "What happened to you?"

"He fixed my foot rubber."

"So, that makes him a good guy? Just like that?"

"I don't know," she said, uncertainly. She seemed

to reconsider for a second. "I guess. Come on, let's go home."

Two weeks later, Sherman had said nothing more about himself, responding only to trivial questions put to him. He did however repair or make better every machine in the restaurant. He had fixed the toaster oven, the gas lines of the big griddle, the dishwasher, the phone, the neon OPEN sign, the electric-eye buzzer on the front door, the meat slicer, the coffee machine, the manual mustard dispenser, and the cash register. Douglas found the man's skills invaluable and wondered how he had ever managed without him. Still, his presence was disconcerting as he never spoke of his past or family or friends and he never went out, not even to the store, his food being already there, and so Douglas began to worry that he might be a fugitive from the law.

"He never leaves the shop," Sheila complained. She was sitting in the passenger seat while Douglas drove them to the movie theater.

"That's where he lives," Douglas said. "All the food he needs is right there. I'm hardly paying him anything."

"You pay him plenty. He doesn't have to pay rent and he doesn't have to buy food."

"I don't see what the trouble is," he said. "After all, he's fixed your massage thingamajig. And he fixed your curling iron and your VCR and your watch and he even got the squeak out of your shoes."

"I know. I know." Sheila sighed. "Still, just what do we know about this man?"

"He's honest, I know that. He never even glances at the till. I've never seen anyone who cares less about money." Douglas turned right onto Connecticut.

"That's exactly how a crook wants to come across."

"Well, Sherman's no crook. Why, I'd trust the man with my life. There are very few people I can say that about."

Sheila laughed softly and disbelievingly. "Well, don't you sound melodramatic."

Douglas really couldn't argue with her. Everything she had said was correct and he was at a loss to explain his tenacious defense of a man who was, after all, a relative stranger. He pulled the car into a parallel space and killed the engine.

"The car didn't do that thing," Sheila said. She was referring to the way the car usually refused to shut off, the stubborn engine firing a couple of extra times.

Douglas glanced over at her.

"Sherman," she said.

"This morning. He opened the hood, grabbed this and jiggled that and then slammed it shut."

The fact of the matter was finally that Sherman hadn't stolen anything and hadn't come across in any way threatening and so Douglas kept his fears and suspicions in check and counted his savings. No more electricians. No more plumbers. No more repairmen of any kind. Sherman's handiness, however, did not remain a secret, in spite of Douglas's best efforts.

It began when Sherman offered and then repaired a small radio-controlled automobile owned by
a fat boy.

The fat boy, who wore his hair in braids, came
into the shop with two of his skinny friends. They sat
at the counter and ordered a large soda to split.

"This thing is a piece of crap," the fat boy said. His
name was Loomis Rump.

"I told you not to spend your money on that thing,"
one of the skinny kids said.

"Shut up," said Loomis.

"Timmy's right, Loomis," the third boy said. He
sucked the last of the soda through the straw. "That's
a cheap one. The good remote controls aren't made of
that thin plastic."

"What do you know?" Loomis said. Loomis pushed
his toy another few inches away from him across the
counter, toward Sherman. Sherman looked at it, then
picked it up.

Douglas was watching from the register. He observed as Sherman held the car up to the light and
seemed to smile.

"Just stopped working, eh?" Sherman said to the
boys.

"It's a piece of crap," Loomis said.

"Would you like me to fix it?" Sherman asked.

Douglas stepped closer, thinking this time he might
see how the repair was done. Loomis handed the remote to Sherman. Douglas stared intently at the man's
hands. Sherman took out his pocketknife and used
the small blade to undo the Phillips-head screws in

order to remove the back panel from the remote control. Then it was all a blur. Douglas saw nothing and then Sherman was replacing the panel.

"There you go," Sherman said and gave the car and controller back to Loomis.

Loomis Rump laughed. "You didn't even do nothing," he said.

"Anything," Sherman corrected him.

Loomis put the car on the floor and switched on the remote. The car rolled away, nearly tripping a postal worker, and crashed to a stop at the door. It capsized, but its wheels kept spinning.

"Hey, hey," the skinny boys shouted.

"Thanks, mister," Loomis said.

The boys left.

Fat Loomis Rump and his skinny pals told their friends and they brought in their broken toys. Sherman fixed them. The fat boy's friends told their parents and Douglas found his shop increasingly crowded with customers and their small appliances.

"The Rump boy told me that you fixed his toy car and the Johnson woman told me that you repaired her radio," the short man who wore the waterworks uniform said.

Sherman was wiping down the counter.

"Is that true?"

Sherman nodded.

"Well, you see these cuts on my face?"

Douglas could see the cuts under the man's three-day growth of stubble from the door to the kitchen. Sherman leaned forward and studied the wounds.

"They seem to be healing nicely," Sherman said.

"It's this damn razor," the man said and he pulled the small unit from his trousers pocket. "It cuts me bad every time I try to shave."

"You'd like me to fix your razor?"

"If you wouldn't mind. But I don't have any money."

"That's okay." Sherman took the razor and began taking it apart. Douglas, as always, moved closer and tried to see. He smiled at the waterworks man who smiled back. Other people gathered around and watched Sherman's hands. Then they watched him hand the reassembled little machine back to the water-works man. The man turned on the shaver and put it to his face.

"Hey," he said. "This is wonderful. It works just like it did when it was new. This is wonderful. Thank you. Can I bring you some money tomorrow?"

"Not necessary," Sherman said.

"This is wonderful."

Everyone in the restaurant oohed and aahed.

"Look," the waterworks man said. "I'm not bleeding."

Sherman sat quietly at the end of the counter and fixed whatever was put in front of him. He repaired hair dryers and calculators and watches and cellular phones and carburetors. And while people waited for the repairs, they ate sandwiches and this appealed to Sherman, though he didn't like his handyman's time so consumed. But the fact of the matter was that there was little more to fix in the shop.

One day a woman who believed her husband was having an affair came in and complained over a turkey and provolone on wheat. Sherman sat next to her at the counter and listened as she finished, ". . . and then he comes home hours after he's gotten off from work, smelling of beer and perfume and he doesn't want to talk or anything and says he has a sinus headache and I'm wondering if I ought to follow him or check the mileage on his car before he leaves in the morning. What should I do?"

"Tell him it's his turn to cook and that you'll be late and don't tell him where you're going," Sherman said.

Everyone in the shop nodded, more in shared confusion than in agreement.

"Where should I go?" the woman asked.

"Go to the library and read about the praying mantis," Sherman said.

Douglas came up to Sherman after the woman had left and asked, "Do you think that was a good idea?"

Sherman shrugged.

The woman came in the next week, her face full with a smile and announced that her home life was now perfect.

"Everything at home is perfect now," she said. "Thanks to Sherman."

Customers slapped Sherman on the back.

So began a new dimension of fixing in the shop

as people came in, along with their electric pencil sharpeners, pacemakers, and microwaves, their relationship woes, and their tax problems. Sherman saved the man who owned the automotive-supply business across the street twelve thousand dollars and got him some fifty-seven dollars in refund.

One night after the shop was closed, Douglas and Sherman sat at the counter and ate the stale leftover doughnuts and drank coffee. Douglas looked at his handyman and shook his head. "That was really something the way you straightened the Rhinehart boy's teeth."

"Physics," Sherman said.

Douglas washed down a dry bite and set his cup on the counter. "I know I've asked you before, but we've known each other longer now. How did you learn to fix things?"

"Fixing things is easy. You just have to know how things work."

"That's it," Douglas said more than asked.

Sherman nodded.

"Doesn't it make you happy to do it?"

Sherman looked at Douglas, questioning.

"I ask because you never smile."

"Oh," Sherman said and took another bite of doughnut.

The next day Sherman fixed a chain saw and a laptop computer and thirty-two parking tickets. Sherman, who had always been quiet, became increasingly more so. He would listen, nod, and fix the problem.

That evening, a few minutes before closing, just after Sherman had solved the Morado woman's sexual-identity problem, two paramedics came in with a patient on a stretcher.

"This is my wife," the more distressed of the ambulance men said of the supine woman. "She's been hit by a car and she died in our rig on the way to the hospital," he cried.

Sherman looked at the woman, pulling back the blanket.

"She had massive internal—"

Sherman stopped the man with a raised hand, pulled the blanket off and then threw it over himself and the dead woman. Douglas stepped over to stand with the paramedics.

Sherman worked under the blanket, moving this way and that way, and then he and the woman emerged, alive and well. The paramedic hugged her.

"You're alive," the man said to his wife.

The other paramedic shook Sherman's hand. Douglas just stared at his handyman.

"Thank you, thank you," the husband said, crying.

The woman was confused, but she, too, offered Sherman thanks.

Sherman nodded and walked quietly away, disappearing into the kitchen.

The paramedics and the restored woman left. Douglas locked the shop and walked into the kitchen where he found Sherman sitting on the floor with his back against the refrigerator.

"I don't know what to say," Douglas said. His head

was swimming. "You just brought that woman back to life."

Sherman's face looked lifeless. He seemed drained of all energy. He lifted his sad face up to look at Douglas.

"How did you do that?" Douglas asked.

Sherman shrugged.

"You just brought a woman back to life and you give me a shrug?" Douglas could hear the fear in his voice. "Who are you? What are you? Are you from outer space or something?"

"No," Sherman said.

"Then what's going on?"

"I can fix things."

"That wasn't a thing," Douglas pointed out. "That was a human being."

"Yeah, I know."

Douglas ran a hand over his face and just stared down at Sherman. "I wonder what Sheila will say."

"Please don't tell anyone about this," Sherman said.

Douglas snorted out a laugh. "Don't tell anyone. I don't have to tell anyone. Everyone probably knows by now. What do you think those paramedics are out doing right now? They're telling anybody and everybody that there's some freak in Langley's Sandwich Shop who can revive the dead."

Sherman held his face in his hands.

"Who are you?"

News spread. Television-news trucks and teams camped outside the front door of the sandwich shop. They were waiting with cameras ready when Douglas showed up to open for business the day following the resurrection.

"Yes, this is my shop," he said. "No, I don't know how it was done," he said. "No, you can't come in just yet," he said.

Sherman was sitting at the counter waiting, his face long, his eyes red as if from crying.

"This is crazy," Douglas said.

Sherman nodded.

"They want to talk to you." Douglas looked closely at Sherman. "Are you all right?"

But Sherman was looking past Douglas and through the front window where the crowd was growing ever larger.

"Are you going to talk to them?" Douglas asked.

Sherman shook his sad face. "I have to run away," he said. "Everyone knows where I am now."

Douglas at first thought Sherman was making cryptic reference to the men who had been beating him that night long ago, but then realized that Sherman meant simply *everyone.*

Sherman stood and walked into the back of the shop. Douglas followed him, not knowing why, unable to stop himself. He followed the man out of the store and down the alley, away from the shop and the horde of people.

Sherman watched the change come over Douglas and said, "Of course not."

"But you—" The rest of Douglas's sentence didn't have a chance to find air as he was once again repeating Sherman's steps.

They ran up this street and across that avenue,

crossed bridges and scurried through tunnels and no matter how far away from the shop they seemed to get, the chanting remained, however faint. Douglas finally asked where there were going and confessed that he was afraid. They were sitting on a bench in the park and it was by now just after sundown.

"You don't have to come with me," Sherman said. "I only need to get away from all of them." He shook his head and said, more to himself, "I knew this would happen."

"If you knew this would happen, why did you fix all of those things?"

"Because I can. Because I was asked."

Douglas gave nervous glances this way and that across the park. "This has something to do with why the men were beating you that night, doesn't it?"

"They were from the government or some businesses, I'm not completely sure," Sherman said. "They wanted me to fix a bunch of things and I said no."

"But they asked you," Douglas said. "You just told me—"

"You have to be careful about what you fix. If you fix the valves in an engine, but the bearings are shot, you'll get more compression, but the engine will still burn up." Sherman looked at Douglas's puzzled face. "If you irrigate a desert, you might empty a sea. It's a complicated business, fixing things."

Douglas said, "So, what do we do now?"

Sherman was now weeping, tears streaming down his face and curving just under his chin before falling to the open collar of his light blue shirt. Douglas watched him, not believing that he was seeing the same man who had fixed so many machines and so many relationships and so many businesses and concerns and even fixed a dead woman.

Sherman raised his tear-filled eyes to Douglas. "I am the empty sea," he said.

The chanting became louder and Douglas turned to see the night dotted with yellow-orange torches. The quality of the chanting had become strained and there was an urgency in the intonation that did not sound affable.

The two men ran, Douglas pushing Sherman, as he was now so engaged in sobbing that he had trouble keeping on his feet. They made it to the big bridge that crossed the bay and stopped in the middle, discovering that at either end thousands of people waited. They sang their dirge into the dark sky, their flames winking.

"Fix us!" they shouted. "Fix us! Fix us!"

Sherman looked down at the peaceful water below. It was a long drop that no one could hope to survive. He looked at Douglas.

Douglas nodded.

The masses of people pressed in from either side.

Sherman stepped over the railing and stood on the brink, the toes of his shoes pushed well over the edge.

"Don't!" they all screamed. "Fix us! Fix us!"

# House

◆

The doctor leaned back, the brown leather upholstery
of his chair visible above his head, smiled, and said,
"And what are you thinking as you look at me now?"

"I'm not thinking anything" Harry House said,
which was not completely true, as he was thinking
that the laundry room must have changed detergents
because his clothes weren't making him itch today.
The light blue pajama pants and pullover shirt usually tortured him, but not today, and he looked at the
doctor and said, "I'm not itching."

The skinny man brought his body forward and put
his elbows on his desk. "This is good, itching? Itching
to what? You're not itching to what?"

Harry knew the man wanted to hear him say that
he was not itching to bash in his face or not itching
to scale the wall and disappear into the poor black
neighborhood on the other side. "My body isn't itching. I think they changed soaps in the laundry. Do you
ever get that? You know, when your skin is so sensi-
tive to stuff?"

The doctor's face fell, the disappointment couldn't

have been more obvious, though he tried to mask it and move on. " Are you still keeping a journal?"

"Of sorts." Harry interlaced his fingers and offered his nails a brief examination, noticing that they were in need of trimming. "It's more a recounting of some memories than it is about my feelings. I know that's not exactly what you wanted."

"That's fine. I'm sure that will be helpful for you as well." He looked at his pad, then made a note with a short, chewed pencil. "The last time we talked you mentioned the death of your brother as being a really bad time growing up."

"Wouldn't it have to be?"

The doctor nodded. "But you said you resented him for dying. I think your words were, 'He found a way to get everyone to look his way.' Just what did you mean by that?"

Harry shrugged. "If I did say that, I didn't feel it. I wouldn't have resented him. Especially since I never wanted anyone paying attention to me anyway. I would have welcomed the diversion."

"Why didn't you want attention?"

"Just didn't." Harry watched the man's eyes, knowing that long ago he had diagnosed him as having schizophrenia. That was how he had overheard the man put it. *The patient has schizophrenia.* For the doctor it was a disease, but for the orderlies and nurses who dealt with him daily, he was *schizophrenic.* For those working on the ward at night when patients peed on the floor and screamed bloody murder, it was a matter of interpersonal etiology.

"Did you love your brother? No, wait, let me put it this way: Did you *like* your brother?"

"Yes." The answer was automatic and a lie only in the sense that Harry could not actually recall a brother.

"Were the two of you close?"

"He was five years older." This was indeed a lie.

"Yes, I know, but my question is, were you close?"

"Not terribly."

"So, you weren't greatly saddened by his death?"

"I guess I don't know what actually constitutes *greatly saddened* in your thinking. My *normal* sadness might put your *great* sadness to shame."

"I see." The doctor tapped his pad with the eraser of his pencil, a rhythmic tapping and Harry began to count them. "You're a bright person, Harry."

"So you tell me."

The doctor poured himself a glass of water from the clear plastic pitcher on his table. "Would you like a drink?" When Harry shook his head no, the man took a sip and asked, "Any dreams lately?"

"No."

"No dreams?"

"I don't dream."

"Everybody dreams," he said.

"I don't."

"Is this a decision you've made? Not to dream?" The doctor leaned back again. Harry could see that the man believed he had lured his prey into some open meadow.

"No more that you've decided *to* dream."

"Well, I think that's enough for today." He looked at his appointment book, which was open on his desk. "I'm on vacation next week, so I won't see you until a week from next Tueday."

Harry nodded.

Harry didn't go to the common room as he usually did to sit and watch televison game shows in which people always appeared a bit green. Instead, he went back to his bed on the ward where he lay on his back and stared at the ceiling, smelled the urine that had collected on the floor of the bathroom just twenty feet away, counted the watermarks on the green walls. He pressed his eyes shut and searched for sleep, tried to remember how it was done, sleeping, was pleased he had lied to the shrink about his dreaming.

It was exceedingly difficult for Harry to find sleep on the ward, what with the snoring of the asthmatic old man in the bed to his right and the more than occasional meeting of one particular orderly and any of several nurses in the empty bed to his left. Tonight, the orderly was grunting away over the short nurse from the medication dispensary. Harry had always liked her and didn't think she would become one of the string, but he could hear her breathing now, could smell her sweat and the orderly's. He could hear her fingernails as she clutched at the bedding and he knew she didn't want to be there, didn't want that hairy orderly inside her and he wondered why she was there then. He knew that the image of her white hose flowing from the mattress to the tiles of the floor would stay with him and also the way her stocky, smooth thighs seemed so clean compared to the hairy legs between them. They were done in just a few minutes, but the sound of it all remained in the room, the mussed sheets seeming to glow in the darkness. Harry had watched them begin, but had then quietly turned away, turned away when for a sharp second the young nurse saw his eyes, saw him watching her, recognizing her.

The following morning as Harry stood at the window to receive the medication, blue and white capsules he never swallowed, the young nurse was abrupt with him, avoiding his eyes, and when he didn't immediately step away from the station, she cut him a keen glance that embarrassed him. He could see beyond her into the office, the venetian blinds slicing the light coming through the window, and there was the orderly, strutting around, all pumped up like a peacock, his open shirt offering a glimpse of chest hair. Harry felt the smooth scars that halfway encirled his forearms, as he sometimes did for comfort. He then stepped away into the middle of the common room. Harry gave his medication to the quiet vet who always sat in the corner near the window, the vet who constantly tapped his foot, chanting, "One, two, three, boom," and then went to sit at the card table with the old man, Harold.

"You know, of course, that I'm God," Harold said, as he always said. "They all pray to me. That's why they say, 'Harold be thy name.' Want to play chess?" Harold didn't wait for a response, but started arranging the pieces on the folding hard-paper board. His pajama top was stained with the morning's breakfast. "You'll be black and I'll be white because, frankly, that's the way it is." He laughed. He said the same thing every day and every day he laughed the same way. Harold pushed his king's pawn forward two squares. Harry made the same move. "Hmmm," Harold said as if the move were some complicated trick, then he giggled like a boy and said, "Did you hear them last night?"

Harry shook his head no.

"You must have. They were right there next to you. He was grunting away over her like a dog." Harold picked up his queen and moved her in spirals through the air before setting her down on the square in front of his king's knight's pawn.

Harry studied the illegal move.

"I bet he's fucked every one of them by now."

"He's a pig," Harry said.

"Well, of course, he is." Harold didn't wait for Harry's response on the board, but moved his king's rook over its pawn, across the board, and captured Harry's king's bishop. "Check. My daughter is a slut. I told her so and she put me in here. I said, 'Doris, or whatever your name is, you are a slut, a S-L-U-T,' and then she and that Nazi boyfriend of hers put me in the back of their Toyota four-wheel-drive piece-of-shit pickup truck and brought me here. They told everyone I was violent and that I wandered off frequently and slept in the street."

Harry took the rook with his king.

"I didn't see that," Harold said. "He's a pig, all right,

that guy, and all these little sluts he porks are his piglets." Harold chuckled. "His piglets. The way he grunts.
He grunts and they squeal." He made a barrage of pig
noises. "It's your move. But I didn't wander off frequently like they claimed. I slept in the street right in
front of their house."

"I'm going to break out of here," Harry said.

"Sure you are. Sure you are. It's your move. Besides,
what would you do out there? Work? You fucked up
and now you belong in here with me, God. God will
take care of you. I'll take care of you and send my
daughter to stinking, sweaty hell where she can cook
burgers for her friends. And another thing, if you were
to 'break out,' as you put it, where would you live? You
never did have any family or so you tell me. Where
would you go? The only place you know is here."

"I'm not crazy."

Harold looked at him. "I know that, but it doesn't
matter. I'm crazy and I can see plain as day that Gillis
over there is crazy and I can see that Greenfeld over
there is crazy and I can even see that our orderly stud
with the short and crooked pecker is nuts, but you're
not crazy."

Harry couldn't tell if Harold was joking.

"I'm a fucking expert on crazy. I know how it hap-
pens and I know what it looks like. Your fucking problem is that you're not crazy. Your fucking problem
is that you're too fucking sane." Harold's cheek was
beginning to twitch the way it did whenever he got
excited, and soon he would be spitting on the floor.
"You're all right and that's why you don't belong out

there. If you go out there, you will be crazy. Look at me," he paused to let Harry find his eyes, "I know."

Harry didn't play basketball out in the yard with the others, it being no fun, crazy people not being very good at games, certainly never understanding or even caring about the rules. With basketball they comprehended that the ball was to go through the hole, but when Harry put the ball through the hole they all got mad and asked why he was in the hospital anyway since he wasn't crazy. So he avoided the basketball court and walked around to the side of the building where the gardeners had planted bearded irises along the walk, but he stayed well within the path because beyond the irises, between the azaleas and the wall of the building, a number of the homosexual inmates sometimes gave each other blow jobs.

Harry walked to the low brick wall above which stood high iron bars like the ones bolted to the windows. He looked at the row of houses across the street, tattered two-story houses that shared walls, only twice in the block were the buildings separated by driveways. A couple of teenagers who were sitting on a stoop pointed his way and shared a laugh and on the street, a couple of houses down, Harry thought he saw a drug transaction. A skinny woman in a crocheted skirt gave money to a man in a mid-seventies Chevy sedan with a vinyl top. Harry would find the other side of this barrier, but he was, of course, afraid and, of course, quite certain that what he would find on the other side would be just room enough to run to the next barrier, and there would be more crazy faces to mock and confuse him. He didn't know how he knew the things he knew, didn't know how it was he recognized place names in the newspaper or how it was he knew the car just pulling away from the skinny woman was a Chevy or how he knew that the skinny woman would suck a cock for ten dollars. He didn't know how he knew that the welds on the wrought-iron bars were sloppy, though more than sufficient to keep him from pushing his way to freedom. A garbage truck rolled by, consigning to the air a momentary stench, and when it was gone so were the teenagers on the stoop and so was the skinny woman and her day's fix, leaving the street empty, cold, lonesome, and desolate, and Harry knew somehow that was the place for him.

Harry was not asleep, a welcome pause from the dreams. He was lying on his bed, smelling the bleach in the sheets, knowing that the old man beside him had wet himself again, knowing because of the way he was not snoring, but whimpering and whispering his dead wife's name. The orderly was making his way down the hall with the heavy nurse with red hair who was the only woman he fucked who truly seemed to like his brutish humping. Her nails twirled the hair on his back and near the end she spat out the word fuck over and over, not as instruction but as exclamation, and once when she was barking out the word, Harry saw her glancing about the ward, even pausing to offer him a brief smile as she caught him looking.

Tonight they fumbled in through the darkness the way they always did, the orderly's sneakers squeaking on the linoleum tiles, their giggling coated with the timbre of a few drinks from the bottle of Jim Beam that everyone knew the orderly kept in his locker. Once, the vet who sat in the corner was caught sneaking a nip from the stash and the orderly punched and kicked him until he bled from his ear. The orderly fell on top of the nurse on the empty bed between Harry and the vet, the frame squeaking as the whole of it scooted across the floor an inch or two, the nurse letting escape a loud and suddenly swallowed laugh. Harry watched them work off their clothes, panting and grunting, the smell of the alcohol wafting over to him, his eyes opened only to slits so that they would not see him watching; not that he was concerned with their discovering him, but he wanted them to assume that he was asleep. Their clothes off, the orderly was on top of the nurse, his fat ass rising and falling and she was staring at the ceiling like she was counting the cracks, but moaning all the while. The orderly's face was buried in her neck and hair on the side away from Harry and so he didn't see when Harry stood up, didn't see when Harry reached under his bed and came back with the unopened can of soda pop that he had gotten from the canteen earlier that day, didn't see when Harry raised it high over his head, but the nurse saw, her eyes growing wide, her mouth opening without a sound, and perhaps because she stopped moving or stopped breathing, the orderly began to come up. Harry brought the can down onto the back of the orderly's head with the force of a baseball pitch, striking just below the bald spot, the dull thump of the blow not sounding real, the repercussion of it shooting through his arm to his chest, and the target fell limp over the woman, still motionless, still voiceless. Harry waited for the orderly to move, poised to strike again, but the orderly didn't move and so Harry put down the can on his bed, picked up the man's trousers from the floor, and stepped into them, pulling the cloth belt tight as the waistband gathered around his middle. He put his fingers to his pursed lips, signaling the nurse to be quiet, and she nodded. He then pulled the orderly's smock over his head and felt for the ring of keys in the pant pockets.

Harry stepped down the hall away from the ward and to the first door and, after trying a couple of keys, had it open and locked behind him. To his surprise, his heart was not racing and this fact alone was exhilarating. He was in the familiar corridor of the doctors' offices, where every Tueday and Thursday for the last too-many-to-remember years he had met one shrink and then another, a string whose faces and names had all run together, all offering up the same assessment that Harry was fairly bright, possessing an overly active ability for detecting irony, which Harry found ironic, and was without doubt paranoid and certainly schizophrenic.

There was one guard at the door, a fat man whom Harry had never before seen, a black man with his hair done in braids, sitting behind the desk that he made appear small. He was drinking diet soda from a two-liter bottle and then holding the plastic vessel in his lap while he watched the little television that sat on the corner of the desk. Every several seconds he belched out a high-pitched laugh and then sucked down more soda pop. Harry waited, crouched down behind a broad-leafed plant about thirty feet down the hall. The lights were dimmed and Harry managed to make it to the door of the public lavatory another fifteen feet closer to the exit doors without being detected. He removed the key he had used to unlock the ward door, then threw it as far as he could down the hall away from the guard's station. Behind the closed door of the restroom, Harry could hear the fat man groan to his feet, then the heavy falls of his boots toward him and past. The man was well down the corridor when Harry opened the door and peeked, and he took that time to move quickly to the front door.

Harry got to the door, that familiar institutional door, the kind he had run to at the end of the day in grade school, the kind he had opened for his mother after his father was pronouced dead at Jackson Memorial, the kind they have at the DMV and the sports arena, the kind that you can always open from the inside by pressing the long bar. He opened the door to the chilly air, but he didn't pause to let it intoxicate him, he pushed on, letting the door quietly to, and then ran across the circular drive lined with empty parking slots and down the walk to the street. Now his heart was racing, his slippers not thick enough to quiet the

sting of the asphalt as he sprinted across the street.
His breath was gone and though he hadn't run very
far, he could run no farther and he sat on the first
stoop he found and stared back at the facility from
which he had just escaped.

Harry watched as an ambulance rolled through the
circular drive, lights flashing but without a siren, up
to the door of the hospital and he wondered if he had
perhaps killed the hairy orderly. A couple of police
cars followed, with lights and also no sirens, but Harry
made no move to his feet, just looked on as car doors
opened and slammed shut and people ran into the
building.

"Hell of a lot of commotion," a deep voice came
from the door behind him.

Harry looked back and saw a smallish man with
gray hair and a gray beard and dark glasses standing
behind the screen. "I guess."

"Some loon probably tried to hang himself with
dental floss or something," the man said.

"I hope you don't mind me sitting on your stoop."

"Are you a robber?"

"No, sir."

"Then I don't mind." The man tilted his head
slightly. "Can you tell me what's going on over there?"

Harry didn't understand the question. How was
he to know what was happening over there? Then it
dawned on him that the man had maybe seen him
escaping. "I don't know."

"Just tell me what you're seeing."

Harry studied the man, the way he seemed to stare

at nothing, the way he tilted his head, and Harry came to the determination that the man was blind. "Well, there's an ambulance from Mercy Hospital and a couple of cop cars. The lights are flashing and sweeping the grounds and the empty parking lot with red and blue."

"Thank you. You did that very nicely."

Harry stood up, keeping his eye on the people gathered in front of the hospital and said, "Well, I guess I'd better keep moving. And thanks for the use of your stoop."

"Good night," the old man said and then he closed the door.

Harry glanced back and saw the stretcher being brought out with the orderly laid out on it, his face uncovered and leading Harry to believe that the man was still alive, though from a hundred yards he looked none too good. As he stepped away from the stoop he looked back and saw that there was space under the steps, a space big enough for him to crawl into, a place to hide, to sleep. He thought the police would be looking for him soon and that the last place they would search would be across the street from the hospital. He got down on the ground and squeezed into the space, tried to fold himself into as small a ball as possible, trying to use his own body heat to get warm, rubbing his arms and legs. He closed his eyes and knew that the dream would continue, knew that he couldn't stop it.

# Alluvial Deposits

◆

People are just naturally *hopeful,* a term my grandfather used to tell me was more than occasionally
interchangeable with *stupid.* So hopeful were people
attempting to tame the arid plains of the West they
believed that rainfall would be divinely moved to in-
crease with their coming, that rain followed the plow.
Law was at one time you had to plant one quarter of
your section in timber, the thinking being that trees
increased rainfall. Of course the timber stands did
nothing to make the land wetter and served mainly
to provide activity for settlers when crops would not
grow, that being clearing fallen trees, the steady, powerful wind being the only predictable meteorological
event of the great basin and plains.

Indians accepted the natural condition of things
and so were nomadic, going to where water, food, and
agreeable climate promised to be. The settlers, refin-
ing and reaffirming the American character, preferred
to sit in one place and wait for nature to change. To
sit still for so long required food. To raise food, they
needed land. Since 160 acres of Western land could
support only five cows, they needed more land. More

land, more cows. More cows, more money. More money, more land. More land by hook or crook, usually by adhering to the letter and not the spirit of the law. More land, more cows, more people, no water.

There I was, driving through southern Utah, as dry as it was a hundred years ago, but having benefited from the ambitious efforts of polygamists to irrigate anything flat. A remarkable job, but canals and ditches don't *make* water. And if you pump it out of the ground faster than it fills, then the aquifer soon becomes almost empty, or as the *hopeful* like to say, "not very full at all." I'd driven from Colorado to do some contract work for the Utah Department of Agriculture and the Fish and Game Commission, to perform flow-projection analyses on a couple of creeks. For all the anxiety over water and too little water and no water, all the complaining and worrying, not many people want to be hydrologists.

In order to carry out my first business at the confluence of Talbert and Rocky creeks I had to get the signature of a woman named Emma Bickers for permission to cross her property to get to where I needed to be. The woman lived at the bottom of the mountain in the town of Dotson. She had been sent the form requesting her signature by Fish and Game, but it had been mailed back unsigned. To save time, I would ask her to sign the form and then finish my work in *hopefully* two days.

◆

I pulled into a gas station and stepped out to fill my tanks. A skinny fellow with wild red hair watched me from the diesel pump and folded a stick of gum into his mouth. The afternoon sun was bright but the air was pretty cold, the wind steady.

"You ain't from around here," he said.

"Pretty good," I said. "Was it my Colorado tags or the fact that you've never seen me before that tipped you off?" I put the nozzle into my front tank.

"Nice truck," he said.

"Thanks, I like it." He didn't say anything. I moved to my rear tank and continued to pump gas. "Maybe you could tell me where Red Clay Road is."

"Keep on out this road here, past the motel, past the Sears catalog store, two streets on the left." He folded another stick of gum into his mouth. "What you want over there?"

"Nothing. I was just wondering where it was. Such a pretty name for a road. Red Clay."

"You're a funny guy."

"That's me." I finished with the gas, replaced the nozzle, and then gave him thirty-five dollars. "Gas is high around here."

"Always going up."

"Well, thanks." I climbed in behind the wheel and he walked to my window. "What is it?" I asked.

"Yeah, this is a nice truck."

I nodded, started my engine, and drove away.

Dotson was a small town without threat of becoming a city. The nearby molybdenum mine that had spurred the growth of the town, had died and taken the downtown and all promise of prosperity with it. The main drag was now a row of boarded-up storefronts, but it was close. For reasons too familiar and too tiresome to discuss, I was a great source of interest as I idled at the town's only traffic signal. I followed the gas-station man's directions to Red Clay Road and turned the only way I could.

I parked and walked the twenty-yard dirt path to the front door where I gave a solid but polite knock. A woman yelled for me to come in and so I did. I was met by a fluffy, purring white cat and reached down to pet it. The chill of the April air outside was lost and I found myself growing uncomfortable in my coat. The heater or a fire was roaring somewhere. An old woman of medium height and an angular face appeared at the end of the hall and she stared at me as if I was naked. I stood up from the cat and asked, "Are you Mrs. Bickers?"

She just stared.

"I thought I heard someone say come in."

"Well, you can just get on back out." She took a half-step toward me.

"Ma'am, I'm from the State Department of Agriculture and the Fish—"

She stopped me with her staring and I began to understand what was going on.

"Okay." I backed through the doorway and onto the porch. She was at the door now. "Ma'am, I need your signature on this—"

But she slammed the door and managed to squeeze the word *nigger* through the last, skinniest gap.

I sighed and walked back to my truck.

I don't get mad too much anymore over shit like that. It doesn't make me happy, but it doesn't usually make me mad. It doesn't do any good to get mad at a tornado or a striking snake; you just stay clear. But I couldn't really stay clear. I needed her signature, probably especially now. Who knew how many mis-shapen offspring she might have roaming that blasted mountain with no more elk to hunt. My next stop would have to be the sheriff's office to see if I could get some help obtaining the woman's scrawl.

◆

As much as I love the West, the character of its conten-tious dealings with the rest of the country has been defined by a few rather than the many. The few being a self-serving, hypocritical lot who complain about the damn welfare babies of the cities and take huge sub-sidies to not plant crops and to make near free use of public lands to raise cattle where, if there were a god, no cattle would ever be found. But Westerners, per-haps a function of living in such a harsh landscape, perhaps a function of living in such isolation and dis-tant interdepedence, stick together and so, blindly, the desires of the few become the needs of the many. A man with one section and five sickly cows is a cattle-man just the same as a man with four thousand head and a lease on a hundred thousand acres of BLM land. But damn it's a pretty place.

◆

I drove back to the main street with the intention of returning to the gas station and asking where the sheriff's office was, but I spotted it on my way. I parked in a diagonal space and walked up the concrete steps and inside. The deputy was a big man, even sitting, and he watched me coming toward his desk.

"What can I do you for?" he asked.

"I need some assistance." I produced my papers from the Department of Ag and Fish and Game. "I'm supposed to go up and perform some tests on Rocky and Talbert creeks. I've got to get Emma Bickers' signature on this piece of paper so I can take my readings and go home."

"So, go get it. Her address is right here."

"I tried. It seems she has a bit of a problem with my complexion."

The deputy observed my complexion. "Yeah, I can see. I think you've got a pimple coming on." He laughed.

I didn't, though I appreciated his attempt at humor and his demonstration of something other than sheer amazement that I was there.

He picked up the phone and dialed. "Mrs. Bickers? This is Deputy Harvey . . . ma'am? . . . yes, he's fine . . . ma'am, I've got a fella here from Fish and Game who needs you to sign a paper . . . yes, ma'am, that would be him . . . well, yes, but I think it won't hurt for you to sign . . . just going to check the water in the creeks . . . yes, ma'am . . . yes, ma'am . . . I reckon, they'll get a court order and he'll get to go up there anyway . . . yes, ma'am." The deputy hung up and looked at me.

"Well?"

"She said she'll sign it, but you can't come in."

◆

I stepped into the air. It was nearly four and I was hungry. There was a restaurant across the street and so I left my truck where it was and went in and sat at the counter. There were a couple of men sitting at a booth in the back. They gave me a quick look and returned to their conversation. The menu was written on poster boards over the shelves on the wall facing me.

"Coffee?" the waitress asked. She was a pie-faced young woman with noticeable, but not heavily applied, makeup. She held her blond ponytail in her hand at her shoulder while she poured me a cup. "Know what you want?"

"You serve breakfast all day, like the sign says?"

"All day long, every day," the waitress said.

"Are the hotcakes good?"

"They're okay," she said. Then, quietly, "I wouldn't eat them."

"Eggs and bacon?"

She nodded. "Toast or biscuit?"

"Toast?"

She nodded. "I'll bring you some hash browns, too."

"Thank you, ma'am,"

She moved to the window and stuck the ticket on the wheel, then talked to me from the coffee machine where she seemed to be counting filters. "Visiting or just passing through?"

"I'm working for Fish and Game, doing some work up mountain."

"What kind of work?"

"Checking the streams, that's all."

"We used to go up that mountain all the time when I was a kid. My daddy taught me to fish there." She came back over and wiped the counter near me. "It was good fishing then."

"What about now?"

"I don't know really. I hear tell it's not good like it used to be." She looked over at the men in the booth. "You all right back there?"

"Fine," one of them said.

"You don't go up there anymore, eh?" I asked.

"Nobody does, really," she said.

"Why's that?"

She shrugged.

A hand reached through the window and tapped the bell, then put a plate down. The waitress stepped over, grabbed it, and brought it to me. "You want ketchup or anything?"

"Tabasco?"

She gave it to me.

A couple of young men came in and sat at the opposite end of the counter. "Hey, Polly," one of them said.

"Hey, Dillard." She slid along the counter toward them.

She and the men ignored me while I ate and I liked that just fine. I finished, paid the tab, and left a generous tip, figuring I'd be eating there again.

◆

Emma Bickers' house looked no more inviting than it had earlier. I walked the dirt path to the porch and before I could knock, two loud pops hurt my ears and I could feel the door move, though I wasn't touching it. I looked at the glass high on the door and saw the small holes. I ran back to my truck, keeping low, my heart skipping. I fumbled with my keys, finally got my engine going, and kicked up dust as I sped away. I don't like being shot at, always have a really bad reaction to it. I don't get scared as much as I get really mad. I stayed hunched in my seat until I was well on the main road again.

◆

I parked in the same space and burst into the sheriff's office. The sheriff was standing beside the deputy and they turned to observe me. I was fit to be tied. "That old lady is crazy as hell and I want her arrested."

"What happened?" the sheriff asked.

"That nut shot at me. I hadn't even knocked on the door and she fired two shots."

"Slow down," the sheriff said. "Who are you and who shot at you?"

"This is the guy from Fish and Game I told you about," the deputy said.

"Mrs. Bickers shot at you?" the sheriff asked.

"I don't know for sure. I was on the other side of the door and when the shooting started I took off. I didn't see if anyone opened the door once I was running."

"Harvey, call over to that old biddy's house and find out what the hell is going on," the sheriff said. Then to me, "Are you all right?"

"I'm not shot."

"Well, that's a good thing." He seemed even-tempered, but of course he hadn't been the target. He ran a hand through his graying hair and watched the deputy hang up the phone.

"No answer," Harvey said.

"Why don't you ride on out there and see what in hell's the matter," the sheriff said to Harvey. "And take that gun away from her before she shoots somebody I give a damn about."

"I'm going with him," I said.

"I don't think that's a good idea, Mr.—"

"Hawks," I said.

"Mr. Hawks. Let Harvey get things unraveled."

The sheriff was reasonable in his request, but I was hot. "Listen, all I want is this paper signed so I can do my damn job."

"Let Harvey take the form and get it signed."

"No, I want to watch her sign it. I want her to see me watching her sign it. I'm going with Harvey."

The sheriff sighed. "I don't see why you don't trespass on her land and get it over with."

"With all due respect, sheriff, greetings around here are somewhat unpredictable and I would prefer to keep things as simple and clean as possible." I wasn't backing down.

"I see your point. Harvey, see to it that Mr. Hawks doesn't get killed."

"I'll do my best," Harvey said.

The sheriff looked out the window. "Wait a second. It's too dark to go messing around over there tonight. If she can't see you, Harvey, she might shoot again." The sheriff looked at me. "You gonna press charges?"

"Probably not. Not if she signs this form and not if I get to see her do it."

The sheriff glanced at Harvey and blew out a breath.

"Harvey will pick you up in the morning from the motel across the street. How's that?"

I nodded.

The sheriff walked away, shaking his head, saying, "I hate this fuckin' job. I want to shoot every idiot who voted for me."

Harvey sat at his desk. "I guess I'll see you in the morning then."

◆

I checked into the motel, which was like any motel anywhere, the same room, the same bed, the same synthetic blanket, the same television with cable, and the same fat clerk in slippers holding a scruffy cat with a terrier standing in the doorway behind him.

I threw myself onto the bed, switched on the television, and settled on CNN. I must have fallen asleep fairly quickly because I couldn't recall any of the so-called news when I was awakened by a crash. Then there was shouting. A man's voice, booming, not so much angry as frustrated.

"I'm telling you it's not my fault," the man said.

I couldn't hear the response.

"Her tire was flat and I offered to change it. When I turned around she had her shirt off."

There was another crash. Then a silence.

"I'm sorry if you think that, but I didn't have any interest in her," he said.

Silence.

"I did *not* know her!"

"—"

"That's not true!"

"——"

"Lord Christ, Muriel! Have you lost your mind!
Now, honey, you put that down. Muriel!"

A door slammed. I went to the window and peeked
out. A bearded man wearing jeans and no shirt was
standing in the parking lot, under a bright lamp, looking at the door. His shoulders were fixed in a shrug.
The woman was out of the room, too, her back to me,
a parka covering what I took to be her naked body; an
assumption I made observing her bare feet and legs.
She was waving a large and nasty hunting knife.

"Now, Muriel!"

The woman said nothing. She stowed the knife
under her arm to free her hands for signing something to the man, then pulled her hair away from her
head and let it fall. I, of course, had no idea what she
was saying, but the tone of her signing was clear.

"Quiet down, honey."

"——"

"That's just not true," he said. "Muriel, she's fat.
For chrissakes, she was gigantic. And ugly. I was just
changing her tire."

But apparently Muriel didn't think she was fat and
ugly enough because she threw the knife at the man
and marched into the room, slamming the door. The
man picked up the blade, which had bounced to a
stop well in front of him. He saw me watching and offered a half-smile as if embarrassed.

I left the window and stepped into the shower.

◆

Though I had studied water most of my adult life, I could never quite believe the fact that there is never really any *new* water. Water falls, drains, flows, evaporates, condenses, falls. The same water, different states. That thought can be unsettling, given what we do to water, what we rinse with it, what we put into it. The tailing ponds of the mine up on Blood Mountain were dug into rock, but still the water leeched into the ground, finding the tributaries, finding the creeks, rivers, reservoirs, pastures, spigots.

◆

As I dried with a painfully thin towel I discovered I was again hungry, realized that I should have ordered the hotcakes after all because, though they might have been bad, I would at least still be full. It was not gnawing, belly-stinging hunger, but worse, it was boredom hunger, the kind of hunger that can make a thirty-eight-year-old man fat. But when you're bored in Dotson, Utah, with the Cartoon Network, Larry King, and the people in the next room, you either eat or drink. I decided to eat.

I went to the same restaurant with my heart set on hotcakes. The place was busier, as it was supper time. There were *three* men in the booth in the back. I again sat at the counter. Young Polly had been replaced by what she was bound to become, a forty-year-old, wasp-waisted woman made up to hide what years of wearing too much makeup had done.

"Coffee, hon?"

I looked into the tired eyes. The coffeepot was in her mitt and she was staring right through me, but the "hon" was sincere, however frequently used. I turned my cup over and said, "Please."

"Any idea yet?" she asked.

"I hear the hotcakes are pretty good. I'll have a short stack."

"Coming up."

I heard the bell on the door and felt a blast of chilly air and before I knew it, there was someone seated to the right of me at the counter. It was the bearded man from the parking lot. He had on a T-shirt now, but still no jacket.

"Cold as hell out there," he said, slapping his arms and blowing into his hands. He had a tattoo on his arm of a moon smoking a cigar with the caption: *Bad Moon Raising.*

He caught me staring at his tattoo. I said, "Shouldn't that say—"

He stopped me. "I know, I know. Pissed me off when I found out." He studied his arm for a second. "My girlfriend, Muriel, told me. She laughed at me. You ever been laughed at by a deaf person? And then she called me a—" He made a sign over the countertop.

"What's that mean?"

"I can't say it, but it's offensive." He made the sign again.

"None of that language in here," the waitress said, coming at us with the coffee. "Turn your cup over, Tim. I ain't got all night."

Tim did as she asked and smiled at her while she poured. "Why don't you and me run away, Hortense?"

"So I can have that crazy girlfriend of yours track me down like an animal?" Hortense asked.

Tim shook his head.

"You live in the motel?" I asked.

"House burned down," Tim said and sipped his coffee. "Staying there until we can get back in." He called down to Hortense, "Tell Johnny to slap me on a grilled cheese."

"Grilled cheese!" Hortense called back into the kitchen.

"I heard the son of a bitch," Johnny said.

"Colorful place, eh?" Tim asked, offering his smile to me.

"Slightly."

"What are you doing here? Forest Service?"

I looked at him. "Why do you say that?"

The waitress brought my hotcakes and stepped away.

He looked me up and down. "Give me a break. Khakis, double-pocket shirt with the flaps, lace-up boots. Halfway-intelligent eyes. You're black."

"Lot of black guys in the Forest Service?" I asked.

"Don't know, but black people don't generally show up in Dotson." He put some sugar in his coffee.

"Anyway, I'm from Fish and Game," I said.

"Same difference." He grabbed a napkin from the dispenser and fiddled with it. "Sorry about all the commotion earlier. So, what are you doing here? Counting elk, deer? Redneck poachers?"

"Looking at water, that's all. I'm a hydrologist." I offered my hand. "My name is Robert Hawks."

"Tim Giddy, pleased to meet you."

"So, what do you do, Tim?"

"Everything. I chop wood, build sheds, drive heavy

machinery. But there ain't no more heavy machines around here. No building."

"Why's that?"

"You ain't looked real close at your map. There is one road that leads into Dotson and it don't go nowhere else. It leads out of town for a few miles on the other side and turns into an old mining road. This town was built for the mine and the mine is dead." Tim's sandwich arrived and he took a quick bite, wiped his lips with his napkin, and talked while he got the food situated in his mouth. "We're a dead town, mister."

"Rest in peace," I said.

Tim laughed loudly, calling attention from the three men in the booth. "That's funny. Rest in peace. I like you. You're all right. Rest in peace." He took another bite. "So, we got a water problem or something? Our wells drying up?"

"No, nothing like that. I'm just here to measure the flow of the creeks. Nothing special."

"We sure had enough snow this year," Tim said.

I nodded.

"You know, Muriel's awright. She's just a little high-spirited." Tim polished off the last bite of the first half of his sandwich.

I watched him chew. "High-spirited," I repeated his words and considered them. "She looked like she wanted to kill you."

"Aw, that little ol' knife? She didn't mean nothing by that." Tim got Hortense's attention and pointed to his empty cup. "I just wish I knew what the hell she was signing at least half the time. She gets to going so fast."

"Well, Tim, it was a pleasure meeting you, but I need some rest." I put money on the tab and slid it to Hortense while she filled Tim's cup. "Maybe I'll see you again."

"G'night."

I put myself to sleep as I always did, by imagining myself on a stream, fishing. That night I was on the Madison, fishing a stretch of pocket water that no human had ever seen before. It was about six in the evening in early August, a slight breeze, not too hot. There was no hatch activity and so I was fishing terrestrials off the far bank. I was letting cinnamon ants fall off the weeds into the water. I would cast, let the ant drift, and pull it back before it could get to a fat eighteen-inch brown I could see in the shallows. I wanted the fly to float to him just right. I casted again and again, until finally there was no drag, the ant simply floated at the end of the tippet with no sign of the slightest disturbance to the water behind it. The fat trout rose, gave the ant a looking over, and ate it. I let him sink with it a few inches and then I set the hook.

◆

It was windy and cold the next morning. A light snow had fallen during the night and left everything lightly dusted. I rode with the deputy in his 4 X 4 rig, and my attention was immediately fixed on the radar unit

between us. It did not look as high-tech as I had imagined. There were a couple of dinosaur stickers on the
housing.

"I've never seen a radar thing before," I said.

"To tell the truth, it doesn't see much action
around here."

"Not on the way to anywhere, eh?"

"Not that. We just don't care how fast people drive."

I nodded and turned to the window as we veered
onto Red Clay Road.

Harvey looked at me a couple of times and asked,
finally, "Are you going to wait in the car?"

"Hell no."

"I appreciate guts as much as the next guy, but I
don't much want to get shot at either."

"Okay, I'll hang back a few steps."

"Aw, man." He stopped the rig in the same place I
had parked. "Please wait in the car?"

But I was getting out.

As promised I walked three steps behind him up to
the door. He knocked, then knocked again. The door
opened and we both jumped. It was the old lady.

"Give me the paper," Mrs. Bickers said.

"I'm going to have to come inside and talk to you,
Mrs. Bickers," the deputy said. "You shouldn't be shooting at people. You could have killed Mr. Hawks here."

The old woman cut a glance at me. "I didn't know it
was him I was shooting at."

I stepped into the house after the deputy. The house
was freezing.

"You see, ma'am, that there is the problem," Harvey

said. "It could have been me at the door or the post-
man. You could have killed somebody. Why were you
shooting anyway?"

"I got scared," she said.

Harvey slapped his arms together. "What's wrong
with your heat? Your fire go out?"

"I reckon."

"You got any coffee, Mrs. Bickers?" Harvey was
looking around the hall and into the adjacent rooms.

I held off making any noise like I wanted to leave,
but I didn't want to linger there. I wondered why he
wanted coffee.

"Could you make us some coffee?" he asked.

"I guess so," she said. She gave me a hard look. We
followed her into the kitchen. "You can sit there at
the table." She turned on an electric burner beneath
a kettle. "All I got is instant."

"That's fine," Harvey said. "Ain't that fine, Mr.
Hawks?"

"Fine," I said.

"I'm going have to take your pistol, Mrs. Bickers,"
Harvey said, matter-of-factly. He slipped in the line
so casually I had a new appreciation of him. He was
smarter than I had thought and I felt small for having let my preconceptions get the better of me. The
woman complained with her expression and Harvey
went on. "Like I said, Mrs. Bickers, that could have
been anybody at the door. Mr. Hawks here wasn't trying to break in or nothing, he was just doing his job.
While we're on the subject." Harvey looked to me and
put his hand out and I gave him the form I needed

signed. He flattened the paper on the table, took a pen from his breast pocket, and held it in the air for the old woman. "Right there, ma'am."

Mrs. Bickers took the pen and scratched her name at the bottom of the page. I didn't get the satisfaction from watching her sign that I had imagined. She had the eyes of a cornered animal. I felt sorry for the woman, alone in this cold house, scared of noises, scared of me. Then I felt stupid for giving a damn.

While he folded the paper, Harvey said, "Now, if you could get me that gun." He handed me the form, then looked over at the woodstove, sitting on uneven bricks on the warped linoleum. "Where is the gun, ma'am?"

"It's in my bedroom. I sleep with it."

"I'm going to have to take it," he repeated. "While you're getting it, I'll bring in some wood for your stove."

Mrs. Bickers stared at me for a couple of seconds and then left the room. I had a passing thought she might come back with the pistol and shoot me. She went to her bedroom, returned, and put the gun on the table in front of me. A .22 target pistol. I watched her pour water into two cups, then measure spoonfuls of powdered coffee.

Harvey came in with the wood. "I swear it feels like it's going to let loose with a real storm." He stomped his boots clean on the rug inside the door. He put the logs down and came back to the table, looked at the pistol. "Mercy, Mrs. Bickers, how do you even lift that thing, much less fire it?"

"I do just fine. Here's the coffee." She put the mugs on the table. "You drink, I'll start the fire." She knelt by the stove and began to twist up sheets of newspaper from a plastic crate.

The deputy and I sat and took a couple of sips of the coffee. Finally, Harvey picked up the pistol and popped out the clip, put it in his shirt pocket. "You got any other guns, ma'am?"

"No."

"Just asking."

"I've got to get to work," I said.

"Okay, Mrs. Bickers, we'll be leaving now. Thanks for your cooperation and the coffee and your time."

The woman nodded and followed close behind us toward the front door. We were on the porch, the door was shut. Mrs. Bickers was on the other side.

# True Romance

◆

The problem with the old Jeep was that you had to be sure to park it on a hill if you wanted to start it again. The alternator turned to no decent result and even if it did, the old battery couldn't hold a charge. The flywheel of the starter was so sticky that if you tried to crank it over, a good battery would have drained anyway. Sometimes, finding a hill was a hell of a job. I was okay at my place on the mountain, but when I drove down to Taos, I was in trouble. There was a little slope about a mile from the plaza, outside a business called *The Chicken Lady*. The Chicken Lady, who sold chickens, geese, and ducks, allowed me to park on the hill, all 250 pounds of him. In exchange, I allowed him to put a FOR SALE sign on the windshield of my truck. He loved to dicker about price and tell great lies about its history to Texans and Oklahomans who romanticized such relics.

"Rawley," he said, greeting me as I backed up the hill.

"Chick."

He watched as I set the brake, climbed out, and put my rock in front of the rear tire. "Why don't you get your rig fixed up?" the Chicken Lady asked me. He was holding a big black rooster under one arm and an unlit cigar in his free hand. He looked at the end of the cigar as if surprised it was cold.

"Oh, I don't know," I said. "I don't mind the walk when I come down here. And on the mountain, it's never a problem."

"Seems like a hassle to me," he said.

"What's wrong with a hassle? Besides, I know it's coming."

"Still, the thing looks like hell."

I looked at my truck. "True enough."

The rooster pecked at a button on the Chicken Lady's shirt.

"I'll be back in an hour or so," I said. I watched as he slipped the sign under a wiper. "What if somebody meets your price?"

"It ain't happening," the big man said.

I never much warmed to Taos with all its galleries, which might have been one for all the sameness, with its trendy air and restaurants charging a fortune for what you could buy at the bowling alley for nickels. But the town was there and it had a grocery market better than the convenience store in Questa. It also offered a fly-fishing shop and I guess I owed a thank you to yuppies and the Orvis catalog for that. Before lunch and shopping on my bimonthly visits, I'd stop in and shake the expensive graphite rods and run my fingers along the even more expensive bamboo sticks.

There were always a couple of guys in there engaged in fish talk with the owner.

"I hear they're hitting on stonefly nymphs up in the Box."

"So, what do you think of these new four-hundred-dollar waders?"

To that question, that day, I had to chime in and say, "It'd be a shame to get them wet."

The owner, a squirrely looking fellow despite his pudginess, a bearded transplant from Vermont, shot me a face. He hadn't liked me since I told him I couldn't find a place to fish the Battenkill where I couldn't see a house or a road. And he couldn't believe I actually fished with a turn-of-the-century Abercrombie and Fitch bamboo rod.

I had said to him, "What do you expect me to do? Stick it in some silly display case?" Then I happened to glance up at the wall behind him and saw a 1930 Wright and McGill rod behind glass. Basically, since then he thought I was nuts.

One of the fisher guys said, "Somebody told me there're cutthroat in the Rio Grande."

"That's a myth," Vermont said.

"I ate a myth the other night." I put back the $150 metal fly box. "Fish the confluence of the Grande and the Hondo." Then I thought to have a little fun. "Wait until right after the rafters go by and throw a weighted zug bug behind one of the big rocks."

"That's where you catch cuttthroats?" the man who had brought up the subject asked.

"Browns and rainbows, too. If it's cold enough, you might get lucky and see a flash of red. But, hey, they all taste the same." I tossed the last bit in to get under their skins. I catch and release as much as the next guy, but I despise religions of all kinds.

I left the shop seeming a little like a bully, which was a bad feeling, but like most feelings, I knew it would pass. I was having one of my *what-the-hell-am-I-doing-in-this-stinking-town* epiphanies when a big man threatened to slap handcuffs on me.

"Kiss me first," I said.

Deputy Jack filled most doorways and I felt happy to call him a friend. He fished and camped with me and was always asking to go elk hunting, but I told him gunfire hurt my ears. He said, "Didn't I just see you down here three weeks ago?"

"Out of toilet paper and I figured they must have a lot of it down here. With so many assholes and all."

"A buddy and I are driving over to the Chama on Saturday. Wanna go?"

"I've got to work."

"You don't work," he said.

"It doesn't look like I work."

"You know you ought to just tell people you write that shit. Right now they think you're a pot farmer, or worse, that you're just rich."

"I'm not telling anybody I write romance novels." I glanced up and down the street. "And you promised not to tell anybody either, remember."

"Your secret is safe with me, *Lance*."

"Call me Friday about fishing," I said. "Maybe I will go."

"You bet."

I shopped, then lugged some of my goods back through town. I nodded to a couple of people and responded to offers of rides by shaking my head. The heavy stuff, bags of animal feed and the like, I left to pick up with the truck, motor running all the while. When I got back to the Chicken Lady's, he seemed troubled. I asked what was wrong.

"Remember when you asked me what if somebody met my price?" He was still holding the rooster.

"You didn't sell my truck?"

"No, I didn't do that. But this fella wants it real bad. Says he's making a movie or some shit and, anyway—" Chicken reached into his shirt pocket, pulled out a business card, and gave it to me. "That's the guy's name."

"What's bugging you so bad?" I set my bags in the back of my truck.

"I never had to give in that it weren't my truck before."

"How much did he offer?"

"I hate losing. Even if I'm pretending, I hate losing." The Chicken Lady shook his head.

"How much?"

"He said he'll pay twenty grand for that hunk of shit."

"The guy's a nut. Don't let it bother you, Chick."

"You gonna call him?"

I looked at the card. "Leighton Dobbs," I read the name aloud. "Sounds made up to me. I don't know. I might call him. Do you think I should?"

"Twenty thousand dollars? Hell, yeah."

I moved to fall in behind the wheel. "Are you going to carry that rooster around all day long?"

"He's upset today." The Chicken Lady put a finger to the bird's beak. "His friend died and he's lonely. So, I'm his company."

"Lucky chicken," I said. "You take care now. And thanks."

I arrived home to find my cat and dog stretched out on the porch as if they weren't sure I was coming back. But after an eager lifting of heads to note my arrival, neither got up to greet me.

"Spoiled rotten, both of you," I shouted through the window as I backed into my parking spot.

I put away my supplies, fed the dog and cat, then went out to tend to the horses. I turned my jacket pocket inside out to get rid of loose hay and found the card of the man who wanted my truck. First of all, I couldn't believe the offer and second, I didn't want a crazy person knowing where I lived. As I shoved the card back into my pocket, I lamented the fact that too many crazy people already knew where I lived.

I sat down to write, or at least *type,* some more of my latest, ever-more-like-the-last-one, piece-of-crap novel, this one about an air-traffic contoller and her affair with a pilot who had been seeing two flight attendants on the side. Shelley, that was her name, Shelley, learned about the second affair just as Brad's plane disappeared from the radar on his approach to O'Hare. Writing these things paid my bills and a bit more and I had decided, however much I hated writing them, I wasn't hurting anyone, not even art itself, not even myself. I gave up trying to write serious fiction because I wasn't any good at it. My limitations were unfortunately noted also by my then-wife who took it as a personal affront when I moved to romance.

Writing this stuff always bored me, but bored was bored and it was the same boredom I'd experienced having to talk to corporate fellows I'd guided fishing, the same boredom I'd felt walking irrigation pipelines for ranches and welding shut leaks. The only thing about my job I found amusing was the list I'd receive every couple of months from my editor. The list was of *hot* names. *Shelley* was big again, but it had to be Shelley with an *e-y* and not Shelly with a *y. Brad* and *Lars* were always good. *Brittany, Brandy, Sydney, Lucas,* and *Tasha* were hot. I wanted so much to call my characters *Agnes, Angus, Gertrude,* and *Gisela.*

A couple days later, as I was saddling my mare, a fancy coupe with far too short clearance came creeping up the dirt lane to my place. I left the horse hitched to the post and met the car. A tall, good-looking man got out and so did a tall, good-looking woman.

"Can I help you?" I asked.

But the man had already spotted my truck and was staring at it. I knew that this had to be Leighton Dobbs.

"Are you Rawley Tucker?"

"I am."

"I'm Leighton Dobbs." He shook my hand. "I be-lieve the man with the chickens told you about me."

"He did."

"So, what do you say?"

"It's not a twenty-thousand-dollar truck."

Dobbs smiled at his companion. "Mr. Tucker, this is Devra Filson, my associate."

I nodded a greeting to the woman, then to Dobbs, "I need my truck. I don't want to sell it." As I spoke to them I realized that I knew these people all too well, had seen them before, lunched with them, had drinks with them, had even tried to be one of them, spinning my wheels in L.A. trying to meet the bills by writing screenplays.

Dobbs looked around my property. Though it was neat, it was modest. The barn some fifty yards away was considerably larger and in better repair than the house. I hadn't yet taken down the weeds along the edge of the front pasture, so the place might have seemed a little shabby.

"With twenty thou you could buy a couple of trucks," Dobbs said.

"No doubt. But I like my truck."

"Twenty-three thousand."

"What do you want it for?"

"We're making a film and this is the perfect vehicle."

"The perfect look," Ms. Filson said. Filson then whispered something to Dobbs.

"There are plenty of trucks out there like mine.

Have your makeup people do a job on one. What kind of film are you talking about?"

"It's a feature with a major studio," he said as if I should take note. I didn't take note and he shook it off and went on. "Twenty-five." He and Filson talked without speaking for a few seconds. "Another thing, we might be interested in renting your place here."

"Out of the question." All I wanted to see was their dust.

"Five thou a day for—" he turned to Filson.

"Fourteen or better," she said.

"For at least fourteen days. That's at least seventy thousand dollars."

I whistled. I looked over at my horse and saw she was pawing at the ground. "Listen, my horse is getting antsy. I appreciate the offer, but my answer is no." I smiled at them and turned away.

"You're refusing nearly a hundred thousand dollars?" Filson said.

"Yes, ma'am. I'm happy. I don't need the money. And I sure as hell don't need a bunch of people running around my home. Why do you think I decided to live way up here?"

Dobbs coughed into his fist. "Listen, if you're growing pot or something, we could care less."

"I'm not growing anything. This is my home." Then I said, slowly, "This is where I live."

"Two hundred thousand." Dobbs shifted his weight.

"You don't get it." I stepped closer to them and pointed at the side pasture and the view beyond it. "What do you see out there?"

"I see a nice landscape," Dobbs said.

"Yes, sir. And no people." I pointed to the front pasture. "And there?"

"A couple of horses," Dobbs said.

"And?"

"No people," Filson said.

"How many people do you think your *movie* will bring up here? The crew and the actors and the caterers?"

"Sixty, seventy," he said. "But we'll bring in crews to clean up."

"I won't allow you to mess it up in the first place. I don't know why I'm wasting my time telling you this, because the bottom line is *no*."

Dobbs and Filson were looking at me like I was crazy. "Three-fifty and we'll just be renting the truck."

"Beat it."

I watched them drive away. I mounted and rode to a section of stream I never fished because it was just too pretty. The spot was well above a sharp bend in the flow where the real pot growers in the canyon had repeatedly dammed the creek to divert the water to their crops. For a while I was riding up daily to check the stream and destroy their handiwork. After finding a couple of big fish dead below the dam, I got mad and camped out with my shotgun. I parked myself on a short ridge and waited. I felt like a fool because, in truth, those people scared me, but the Forest Service wouldn't help and Fish and Game just laughed. I saw the sweeping beams of their flashlights in the dawn haze first, then heard their loud talking. Once they had set to work, I fired above them, three shells, then

I moved along the ridge and fired three more, which I'm not sure they appreciated because of their running. My heart was racing and my ears were ringing. I slept there three nights in a row and they never came back.

The water where I stood watching flowed around a couple of boulders and then flattened over a bed of rocks. The pool below held a couple of browns that were at least sixteen inches long. I'd watched them for two years now, getting bigger and fatter and growing accustomed to my presence. They would rise to a hatch if I was standing four feet up the bank.

Deputy Jack drove us over to the Chama early. The morning was brisk, but not cold. The water was high and a little muddy and we weren't sure any fish would find us, but we went at it anyway.

The deputy was in the middle of the river trying to dislodge a fly from a submerged tree, his buddy had wandered downstream, and I was standing at the end of a riffle, bouncing a foam beetle along the bottom.

"That guy find you?" Deputy Jack asked, coming toward me on the bank.

"What guy?"

"That movie fella."

"So, you're the one who told him where I live."

"He asked."

"Do me a favor and don't tell anybody else." I roll-casted to the middle of the riffle and stripped in line. The deputy had his fly and slipped walking back to the bank. "Are you all right?" I asked.

"Yeah, just a little wetter than I'd planned on getting."

"I've got half a mind to try a parachute dragonfly at the top of that riffle." I looked hard at the sunlight bouncing off the broken water. "But then it is just half a mind."

"So, if you hate it so much, why do you write it?" the deputy asked.

"That's an abrupt change of subject."

"It's a trick we cops use. Hardly ever works."

"I write it because I can and I make enough money so that I can live way the hell out here and be happy." I looked at the mountains in the distance. "I don't want to talk about it anymore."

We were quiet for a while, neither of us fishing. The deputy unwrapped a breakfast bar, offered me one. I declined.

"You gonna sell your truck?" The deputy was closer to me, prowling through his fly box. "Lotta money."

"You had a long talk with this guy, did you?"

"Naw. The Chicken Lady told me about the truck and how much the guy's willing to pay. That really shook him up."

"Yeah?" I reeled in my line to check my fly.

"The Chicken Lady doesn't understand how there can be that much money in one person's pocket." Deputy Jack looked up at a circling hawk.

"Yeah, well, I told the guy to take a hike."

"You're crazy."

"Maybe."

"You can pass up that kind of money?" Deputy Jack asked. "Maybe you are growing pot up there."

"I didn't like that guy. I don't want to do business with people I don't like anymore." Which was a lie, because I pretty much hated my publisher, my editor, and my agent.

"You could take my old pickup. Nobody's using it." He folded a stick of gum into his mouth. "It's one of them newfangled jobs. Starts with a key."

"Funny man."

"Just a thought," he said.

"Thanks anyway."

We drove home another way, the *scenic* way Deputy Jack called it. Scenic meant longer and the drive took us into an old town I had always loved, Enrico, through which flowed Enrico Creek. Perhaps sixty people lived in Enrico. The walls of the old buildings were the sides of the road that passed through it. When we reached the other end of the town, I saw an excavated site, a chain-link fence, and a sign announcing the arrival of a Wal-Mart. My heart sank. "What the hell is that?"

The deputy's friend, whose name I couldn't remember, but whose job was repairing firearms, shook his head. "They're blasting open a malachite mine up mountain. Jobs. People. Wal-Mart."

"McDonald's, motels, more people," I said.

No one was working at the construction site, but I caught myself staring at a big yellow grader as if it were a responsible party. I reached down beside me and picked up one of my wading boots. I held it to my nose and inhaled the sour smell of the river water that had soaked the felt sole.

"I'm glad you called," Leighten Dobbs said as he closed his car door. "To tell you the truth I was a little surprised."

I was leading my mare and the fat gelding from the barn to a pasture. I was going to worm them and turn them out. "Here, you can help me," I said.

"How? What?" He looked nervously at the horses.

"Just hold this rope." I gave him control of the mare. He held the rope away from his body as if it were wet. I pulled the tube of worming medicine from my back pocket, grabbed the gelding's nose, and pressed it into his mouth.

"I take it you've changed your mind," Dobbs said.

"About your using my place, yes." I took the mare and had him hold the gelding's lead rope.

"And your truck?"

"You'll have to take that up with the owner. It now belongs to the man you tried to buy it from the first time."

"But it's right there."

"Talk to him tomorrow. The truck will be in front of the store. I promise he'll sell with no problem." I put the paste into the mare's mouth and watched her try to spit it out. I put the empty tube in my pocket. "She hates this stuff," I said. "But we're done. Thanks." I took the gelding.

Dobbs was a bit puzzled, but he nodded. "What

did we decide on for the use of your place? A hundred thousand?" He followed me to the pasture.

"Three-fifty." I opened the gate and led the horses in.

"Oh, yes." He looked around again, at the house, the barn. "Yes, this is it, all right. This is the place I want. It's done."

"I'll need a deposit." I removed the first halter, then the second, and watched the horses trot off.

His smile was an odd one. "Why?"

"So, I'll know you're serious." I closed the gate. "I might change my mind. You never know. You can bring an agreement here with the check tomorrow and I'll sign it."

"Okay," he said.

"And the truck will be in town."

Again, he said, "Okay."

After watching Dobbs head down the mountain, I went inside and called a real estate agent, told him I wanted a list of all the pieces of property for sale in and around Enrico. Tomorrow, I would go to the county clerk's office and find out who owned what. I would buy all I could, where I could, and get in the way of any development.

Early the following morning, I drove down the mountain to Taos and backed onto the Chicken Lady's hill. He met me this time without the rooster under his arm.

"Didn't expect to see you so soon," he said.

"Complaining?"

"Maybe."

"Come on, show me the birds." I followed him through the front gate and into a lath house. Chickens and ducks waddled across the floor, sat on perches, flapped from the rafters.

"Just the plain old birds in here," he said. "Don't get me wrong, they're nice animals and I love them, but they're common." He led the way out of the shaded area and into the backyard. There was a hole in the middle, the digging of which had long been abandoned, the pick and shovel covered with dirt. "I was trying to put me a pond in here for the ducks, but I sprained my back. The ducks are going to love it. It's going to be a sight better than those plastic pools I've been using." He stooped to pick up a black chicken with feathered feet. "This here is a Cochin. She ain't too special, but she's a nice one."

"How many birds do you have?" I asked.

"Don't know." He stopped at a coop with a wire top. "These are my fancy babies. There's a pair of Silver Sussex. That one there is a white Croad Langshan. That breed was almost gone. There's a black Croad. Indian Game. Silver Dorking. You know, I love chickens."

"I know you do, Chick." I looked at his shoes. Black Red Wings with one loose sole. "Thanks for the tour. I'd better get going. Come to my truck with me." We walked back through the lath house, out the gate, and I stopped at the hood of the truck. "Chick, what's your real name?"

"Why do you want to know that?"

"Give me five dollars," I said.

"What?"

"Just give me a five."

The Chicken Lady fished out a lonely five and handed it to me.

"What's your damn name?"

"Iverson P. Mowatt."

"You're kidding me. What's the P for?"

"Peyton."

"That's a great name, Chick."

"Yeah, yeah." He looked at what I was writing. "What are you doing?"

"I'm making out a bill of sale."

"Why?"

"You just bought my truck." I handed him the title and the key. "And here's the card of that movie guy."

The Chicken Lady looked at the bill of sale and the title and the key, then the truck.

"It's okay, Chick. It's your truck now. You can do what you want."

"Thanks, Rawley. I don't know what to say." The big man was starting to mist up.

"Just do me a favor. Hold out for thirty thousand. Okay?"

The Chicken Lady collected himself, stiffened his face, and said, "No problem."

# Age Would Be That Does

◆

It was with some resolve that Rosendo Lapuente put a bullet through the head of his sister's dog, Grasa. Some resolve, a great deal of excitement, and an admirable measure of luck as he dispatched the animal from well over forty yards. Of course it was not until Rosendo and his friend, Mauricio Rocha, were well upon the fallen prey that they realized it was a dog and not until Rosendo's face was mere inches from the canine's head that he recognized it as Grasa.

"Oh my," Rosendo said. "This is your fault."

"It was you who shot him," Mauricio said.

"You told me it was a deer."

"All I said was, 'There, there is one.' I didn't say 'deer.'"

Rosendo studied the dog. "No matter. I've killed my sister's Grasa. *Me siento mareado.*"

*"Respire hondo,"* Mauricio said and sucked in much air and let it out slowly to show what he meant.

"And she's always yelling at me that I'm too old and blind to go hunting. She'll never let me forget *this.*" Rosendo sat on a nearby log and laid the rifle on the ground between his legs.

"*No es para preocuparse,*" Mauricio said.

"How do you figure that?"

"How will she know?" Mauricio asked.

Rosendo sighed. "I suppose you're right. It would be a shame to hurt her with such news." He looked at the dog. "It was a terrible pet anyway, a car chaser. Did you know that?"

"I had heard."

"Bit a hole into the tire of the UPS truck."

"Oh my."

The two friends began their hike out of the forest, saying nothing. Rosendo gave the rifle to Mauricio to carry. They shared the gun and kept it hidden in the shed in back of the house that Rosendo shared with his sister Maria. The men also shared vision; that was how they saw it, Mauricio claiming an ability to see things some distance away and Rosendo saying he could focus on things up close. So, Rosendo did the reading and Mauricio did the driving, having managed to retain his permit by uncannily guessing the letters on the eye chart. Each relied on the other's constant reports. Actually, Mauricio couldn't make out things that far away and Rosendo had to hold large print at arm's length from his face to see that it was indeed print, so it was a safe bet that they saw the same things equally well, or poorly.

They came out of the canyon mouth and found Mauricio's car, a blue Datsun sedan that his daughter, who lived in Albuquerque, had given him when she bought one of those little vans that Mauricio said looked like a suppository. Mauricio wrapped up the gun in a blanket while Rosendo leaned against the car peering at nothing in particular, but in general back into the woods.

"Let me ask you something, Moe," Rosendo said.

Mauricio slammed shut the trunk.

"Do you think we're old?"

Mauricio looked at the same trees. "Hell, Rosie, I know for a fact we're old. We're the oldest people I know. But not like you're thinking. We're young men who still go hunting."

"*Si*, we hunt dogs, pet dogs. What was Grasa doing so far out here anyway?"

The fact of the matter was that they were not very far from Rosendo's home. The house was just a half-mile from the canyon, but Mauricio's driving took them repeatedly over the same dirt lanes and through the same turns. Any trip for Mauricio in his blue Datsun took three times as long as it should have. Walking through the woods was a similar experience for them. Rosendo had killed his sister's dog no more than a hundred yards deep into the woods, but they believed themselves to have marched two or three miles, which they had no doubt done, but in circles. When anyone saw the blue Datsun parked at the canyon opening or anyplace near the mountain, the word was spread to steer clear of the forest.

They parked in the backyard behind the shed and sneaked inside to hide the rifle behind the drums of corn that Maria fed the wild turkeys. The birds were actually guinea hens, but one day Maria had jokingly referred to them as turkeys and Rosendo had said,

"And fine-looking birds they are, too. But, Maria, they don't sound much like turkeys."

"*Hasta luego*, Rosie," Mauricio said, back in his car and waving good-bye to Rosendo as he drove away.

Rosendo took a deep breath and walked through the back door of the house and into the kitchen where Maria was sitting and chatting with Carlita Hireles. "Hello, Maria," he said and proceeded to wash his hands at the sink.

"Aren't you going to say hello to Father Ortega?" Maria said, sharing a smile and a quiet chuckle with her friend.

"I'm sorry, *Padre*, I didn't see you," Rosendo said. He dried his hands on a towel, left it on the counter by the sink, and reached to shake the father's hand.

Carlita lowered her voice and said, "It's good to see you, Rosie."

Rosendo paused at the softness of the hand and then considered it not unlikely that a hand that had never seen manual labor should feel so. "What brings you way out here?" Rosendo asked. "Somebody die?"

"No, no, just saying hello."

Rosendo nodded, knowing as he passed from the kitchen into the living room that he had just spoken to Carlita Hireles. He knew because he recognized the smell of her, perfume and makeup and fancy soap that she bought from the mall down in Santa Fe. They were having a laugh on him, but that was okay, especially today as Grasa wouldn't be showing up for dinner. It was enough that he knew it to be Carlita.

Later, as Rosendo sat eating his dinner of posole,

chiles, and sopaipillas, Maria stood at the screen of the back door looking out for Grasa.

It was then that Miguel Rocha, Mauricio's nephew just out of the army, and Willard Garcia drove into the backyard with much loud noise from their big-wheeled pickup. They came into the house, full of excitement.

"*Que le ocurre?*" Maria asked.

"A lion," Willard said.

"Yes," said Miguel, "there is a cougar around. He killed two sheep over in San Cristobal."

Rosendo listened to them, then stood. "You say there is a lion?"

"*Si*, Rosie." Miguel caught his breath. "From the size of the tracks, a big one, too."

"We're just going around and making sure everybody knows," Willard said. "You know, so people are careful and watch out for their stock and things like that."

"Well, you boys are doing a fine job," Maria said.

"A cat," Rosendo said to himself, sitting again.

Maria took the basket of sopaipillas from the table. "Here, take a couple of these with you," she said.

Each took a couple, thanked Maria, and left.

"Imagine that," Maria said, sitting at the table with Rosendo and shaking her head. " A lion. I hope Grasa hasn't met up with him."

Rosendo chewed a mouthful of posole. "A dog would have little chance against such a beast. Poor Grasa."

The old man finished his meal and went into the living room where he sat and rocked and listened to the radio. He enjoyed particularly the call-in talk shows that had people arguing about such strange things. "That there are such people," he would say, getting up to grab a bran muffin from the basket on the kitchen table. Rosendo stayed up later than Maria, as was his custom, then went to the door and looked out over the yard. The moon was full and Rosendo sensed it more than he saw it. He ate the last bite of muffin and heard a sound. He stopped chewing.

"Rosie," a voice called to him in a whisper.

"Moe? Is that you?"

"*Si.*"

Rosendo listened for movement from Maria's room and finding none, walked out into the yard. "Moe?"

"Rosie?"

"Moe?"

It took the men ten minutes to find each other by sound, but they did. They stood by the shed.

"I didn't hear your car," Rosendo said.

"I parked it down the road. I didn't want to wake up your sister."

"Why have you come here so late?" Rosendo asked.

"I left early, but it was a very long drive. When it got dark the way became even longer."

Rosendo nodded.

"Did you hear about the lion?" Mauricio asked.

"Miguel was here. He told us. There has not been a lion in these parts in many years."

"Miguel and Willard and some of the other men are talking about tracking the animal and hunting it down," Mauricio said. "What do they know about tracking lions, about hunting them? I asked them that and they laughed at me."

"They've never even seen a lion. You and I have seen a lion. Remember?"

"I remember."

"That was a big animal," Mauricio said.

"It killed a bull, I recall that."

"I believe it is we who have to get this monster," Mauricio said.

Rosendo looked back in what he thought was the direction of the house. "I believe you're right. We have to hunt down the lion. But we mustn't tell anyone."

"They would try to stop us for sure."

Rosendo sighed. He then invited his friend to stay the night in his house. "It will be too long a drive for you tonight. We will rise early before Maria wakes up."

Mauricio agreed and retired to the sofa where he slept until first light. Rosendo made sandwiches of chiles and cheese, collected some apples and other foods, filled a couple of canteens, and tied two rolled-up blankets to his knapsack. The men went into the backyard to the shed, where they took their rifle from behind the drums. They found Mauricio's blue Datsun down the road, got in and, after a moderate amount of driving, found the mouth of some canyon.

The two men wandered most of the day, putting distance between themselves and the car by following an arroyo up the mountain. They stopped once to eat and rest, but were driven by great excitement and so moved at a decent clip through the forest. They were serious about their mission, talking little and walking with ears open for noises that might alert them to the cat's presence. Neither had any doubt that they would find the animal. As to what would happen when they did, they were split; Rosendo claiming the right to shoot the lion because he had paid for the shells and Mauricio claiming the same right because the hunt had been his idea. They argued the point off and on, deciding that it just mattered how far away the lion was when the moment arrived. They sat down in a clearing by the creek at dusk and built a small fire. They ate their little wieners from a can with day-old sopaipillas.

"Just like old times, eh, Moe?"

"I can't wait to see their faces when we show up with the lion's head," Mauricio said.

Rosendo pondered this for a few seconds. "The head will be very heavy," he said.

"Perhaps a paw then."

Rosendo nodded. "I wish I had remembered the radio."

"Just something else to carry," said Mauricio as he stood. He stretched his back and legs, then walked some yards away from the fire and into the trees to relieve himself.

Rosendo, who had not noticed his friend's movement, also did not notice that the cougar was now sitting in his friend's place.

"It's cooler out here than I thought it would be," Mauricio called from the trees.

"You sound like you're in a tunnel," Rosendo said.

The lion just sat there and panted.

Rosendo chuckled. "You're getting old, *amigo*. This little walk has fatigued you."

"What was that?" Mauricio asked.

The lion belched.

Rosendo fanned at the odor. "Say 'excuse me.'"

"I'm sorry," Mauricio said. "I didn't know you could hear."

The cougar found its legs quietly and stepped away into the darkness.

Mauricio finished his business and returned to the fire, approaching Rosendo from the other side. "Any more of those wienies left?"

Rosendo jumped at the voice on the wrong side. "What?"

"Did I scare you?"

"How did you do that?"

"Do what?" Mauricio sat down and found the little tin of wieners, took a bite of one. "What are you talking about?"

"Moe, I think the lion was just here. Did you get up and go somewhere?"

"I went back into the trees to take care of some business."

"Hmmm," said Rosendo. "And you were not here beside me?"

Mauricio laughed. "I cannot be in two places at once."

"Let me smell your breath," Rosendo said.

"What is wrong with you?"

Rosendo leaned forward. "Just breathe and let me smell."

Mauricio did.

"Oh my, just as I thought," Rosendo groaned.

"Bad?"

"The lion was here, Moe. He was sitting right beside me."

Mauricio said nothing. The men sat back to back and covered themselves with the blankets, taking turns tossing sticks into the fire. They tried to stay awake. They wondered about things, asked questions like: Did state troopers shift their pistols from hip to hip to avoid becoming lopsided? and, How many yards long was the town of Red River?

"They'd have to," Mauricio said concerning the state-trooper question. "Do you know how heavy those pistols are?"

"I know how heavy they are."

"It would damage their legs if they didn't switch back and forth."

Rosendo shook his head. "People are right- or left-handed. You can't just wear the thing on any side. It has to be on the side of the hand they use."

"They'd end up walking in circles if they didn't switch and even things out," Mauricio said.

"We'll have to find a state trooper and watch him over a period of time," Rosendo said.

Mauricio agreed that that was the way to clear up the matter. That's the way their arguing went, and they didn't know they had gone to sleep until morning came and the birds sang loud songs and squirrels and chipmunks rattled branches.

"Do you think we should continue on up the mountain?" Mauricio asked.

Rosendo looked up the split in the mountain and then down. "What do you think?"

"I think the lion went down."

Rosendo nodded his agreement and that was the way they went, retracing their steps of the previous day.

"There is one thing," Mauricio said.

"What's that?" Rosendo asked.

"We were closer to the beast than anyone else. You were near enough to smell the lion's breath."

"Yes, I was," Rosendo said.

# The Appropriation of Cultures

◆

Daniel Barkley had money left to him by his mother. He had a house that had been left to him by his mother. He had a degree in American Studies from Brown University that he had in some way earned, but that had not yet earned anything for him. He played a 1940 Martin guitar with a Barkus-Berry pickup and drove a 1976 Jensen Interceptor, which he had purchased after his mother's sister had died and left him her money because she had no children of her own. Daniel Barkley didn't work and didn't pretend to need to, spending most of his time reading. Some nights he went to a joint near the campus of the University of South Carolina and played jazz with some old guys who all worked very hard during the day, but didn't hold Daniel's condition against him.

Daniel played standards with the old guys, but what he loved to play were old-time slide tunes. One night, some white boys from a fraternity yelled forward to the stage at the black man holding the acoustic guitar and began to shout, "Play 'Dixie' for us! Play 'Dixie' for us!"

Daniel gave them a long look, studied their big-toothed grins and the beer-shiny eyes stuck into puffy, pale faces, hovering over golf shirts and chinos. He looked from them to the uncomfortable expressions on the faces of the old guys with whom he was playing and then to the embarrassed faces of the other college kids in the club.

And then he started to play. He felt his way slowly through the chords of the song once and listened to the deadened hush as it fell over the room. He used the slide to squeeze out the melody of the song he had grown up hating, the song the whites had always pulled out to remind themselves and those other people just where they were. Daniel sang the song. He sang it slowly. He sang it, feeling the lyrics, deciding that the lyrics were his, deciding that the song was his. *Old times there are not forgotten . . .* He sang the song and listened to the silence around him. He resisted the urge to let satire ring through his voice. He meant what he sang. *Look away, look away, look away, Dixieland.*

When he was finished, he looked up to see the roomful of eyes on him. One person clapped. Then another. And soon the tavern was filled with applause and hoots. He found the frat boys in the back and watched as they stormed out, a couple of people near the door chuckling at them as they passed.

Roger, the old guy who played tenor sax, slapped Daniel on the back and said something like, "Right on" or "Cool." Roger then played the first few notes of "Take the A Train" and they were off. When the set was done, all the college kids slapped Daniel on the back as he walked toward the bar where he found a beer waiting.

Daniel didn't much care for the slaps on the back, but he didn't focus too much energy on that. He was busy trying to sort out his feelings about what he had just played. The irony of his playing the song straight and from the heart was made more ironic by the fact that as he played it, it came straight and from his heart, as he was claiming Southern soil, or at least recognizing his blood in it. His was the land of cotton and hell no, it was not forgotten. At twenty-three, his anger was fresh and typical, and so was his ease with it, the way it could be forgotten for chunks of time, until something like that night with the white frat boys or simply a flashing blue light in the rearview mirror brought it all back. He liked the song, wanted to play it again, knew that he would.

He drove home from the bar on Green Street and back to his house where he made tea and read about Pickett's charge at Gettysburg while he sat in the big leather chair that had been his father's. He fell asleep and had a dream in which he stopped Pickett's men on the Emmitsburg Road on their way to the field and said, "Give me back my flag."

◆

Daniel's friend Sarah was a very large woman with a very large Afro hairdo. They were sitting on the porch of Daniel's house having tea. The late fall afternoon was mild and slightly overcast. Daniel sat in the wicker rocker while Sarah curled her feet under her on the glider.

"I wish I could have heard it," Sarah said.

"Yeah, me too."

"Personally, I can't even stand to go in that place. All that drinking. Those white kids love to drink." Sarah studied her fingernails.

"I guess. The place is harmless. They seem to like the music."

"Do you think I should paint my nails?"

Daniel frowned at her. "If you want to."

"I mean really paint them. You know, black, or with red, white, and blue stripes. Something like that." She held her hand out, appearing to imagine the colors. "I'd have to grow them long."

"What are you talking about?"

"Just bullshitting."

Daniel and Sarah went to a grocery market to buy food for lunch and Daniel's dinner. Daniel pushed the cart through the Piggly Wiggly while Sarah walked ahead of him. He watched her large movements and her confident stride. At the checkout, he added a bulletin full of pictures of local cars and trucks for sale to his items on the conveyer.

"What's that for?" Sarah asked.

"I think I want to buy a truck."

"Buy a truck?"

"So I can drive you around when you paint your nails."

◆

Later, after lunch and after Sarah had left him alone, Daniel sat in his living room and picked up the car-sale magazine. As he suspected, there were several trucks he liked and one in particular, a 1968 Ford three-quarter ton with the one thing it shared with the other possibilities, a full rear cab window decal of the Confederate flag. He called the number the following morning and arranged with Barb, Travis's wife, to stop by and see the truck.

◆

Travis and Barb lived across the river in the town of Irmo, a name that Daniel had always thought suited a disease for cattle. He drove around the maze of tract homes until he found the right street and number. A woman in a housecoat across the street watched from her porch, safe inside the chain-link fence around her yard. From down the street a man and a teenager, who were covered with grease and apparently engaged in work on a torn-apart Dodge Charger, mindlessly wiped their hands and studied him.

Daniel walked across the front yard, through a maze of plastic toys, and knocked on the front door. Travis opened the door and asked in a surly voice, "What is it?"

"I called about the truck," Daniel said.

"Oh, you're Dan?"

Daniel nodded.

"The truck's in the backyard. Let me get the keys." He pushed the door to, but it didn't catch. Daniel heard the quality of the exchange between Travis and Barb, but not the words. He did hear Barb say, as Travis pulled open the door, "I couldn't tell over the phone."

"Got 'em," Travis said. "Come on with me." He looked at Daniel's Jensen as they walked through the yard. "What kind of car is that?"

"It's a Jensen."

"Nice looking. Is it fast?"

"I guess."

The truck looked a little rough, a pale blue with a bleached-out hood and a crack across the top of the windshield. Travis opened the driver's side door and pushed the key into the ignition. "It's a strong runner," he said. Daniel put his hand on the faded hood and felt the warmth, knew that Travis had already warmed up the motor. Travis turned the key and the engine kicked over. He nodded to Daniel. Daniel nodded back. He looked up to see a blond woman looking on from behind the screen door of the back porch.

"The clutch and the alternator are new this year." Travis stepped backward to the wall of the bed and looked in. "There's some rust back here, but the bottom's pretty solid."

Daniel attended to the sound of the engine. "Misses just a little," he said.

"A tune-up will fix that."

Daniel regarded the rebel-flag decal covering the rear window of the cab, touched it with his finger.

"That thing will peel right off," Travis said.

"No, I like it." Daniel sat down in the truck behind the steering wheel. "Mind if I take it for a spin?"

"Sure thing." Travis looked toward the house, then back to Daniel. "The brakes are good, but you got to press hard."

Daniel nodded.

Travis shut the door, his long fingers wrapped over the edge of the half-lowered glass. Daniel noticed that one of the man's fingernails was blackened.

"I'll just take it around a block or two."

The blond woman was now standing outside the door on the concrete steps. Daniel put the truck in gear and drove out of the yard, past his car and down the street by the man and teenager who were still at work on the Charger. They stared at him, were still watching him as he turned right at the corner. The truck handled decently, but that really wasn't important.

Back at Travis's house Daniel left the keys in the truck and got out to observe the bald tires while Travis looked on. "The ad in the magazine said two thousand."

"Yeah, but I'm willing to work with you."

"Tell you what, I'll give you twenty-two hundred if you deliver it to my house."

Travis was lost, scratching his head and looking back at the house for his wife, who was no longer standing there. "Whereabouts do you live?"

"I live over near the university. Near Five Points."

"Twenty-two hundred?" Travis said more to himself than to Daniel. "Sure I can get it to your house."

"Here's two hundred." Daniel counted out the money and handed it to the man. "I'll have the rest for you in cash when you deliver the truck." He watched

Travis feel the bills with his skinny fingers. "Can you have it there at about four?"

"I can do that."

◆

"What in the world do you need a truck for?" Sarah asked. She stepped over to the counter and poured herself another cup of coffee, then sat back down at the table with Daniel.

"I'm not buying the truck. Well, I am buying a truck, but only because I need the truck for the decal. I'm buying the decal."

"Decal?"

"Yes. This truck has a Confederate flag in the back window."

"What?"

"I've decided that the rebel flag is my flag. My blood is Southern blood, right? Well, it's my flag."

Sarah put down her cup and saucer and picked up a cookie from the plate in the middle of the table. "You've flipped. I knew this would happen to you if you didn't work. A person needs to work."

"I don't need money."

"That's not the point. You don't have to work for money." She stood and walked to the edge of the porch and looked up and down the street.

"I've got my books and my music."

"You need a job so you can be around people you don't care about, doing stuff you don't care about. You need a job to occupy that part of your brain. I suppose it's too late now, though."

"Nonetheless," Daniel said. "You should have seen those redneck boys when I took 'Dixie' from them. They didn't know what to do. So, the goddamn flag is flying over the State Capitol. Don't take it down, just take it. That's what I say."

"That's all you have to do? That's all there is to it?"

"Yep." Daniel leaned back in his rocker. "You watch ol' Travis when he gets here."

◆

Travis arrived with the pickup a little before four, his wife pulling up behind him in a yellow TransAm. Barb got out of the car and walked up to the porch with Travis. She gave the house a careful look.

"Hey, Travis," Daniel said. "This is my friend, Sarah."

Travis nodded hello.

"You must be Barb," Daniel said.

Barb smiled weakly.

Travis looked at Sarah, then back at the truck, and then to Daniel. "You sure you don't want me to peel that thing off the window?"

"I'm positive."

"Okay."

Daniel gave Sarah a glance, to be sure she was watching Travis's face. "Here's the balance," he said, handing over the money. He took the truck keys from the skinny fingers.

Barb sighed and asked, as if the question were burning right through her, "Why do you want that flag on the truck?"

"Why shouldn't I want it?" Daniel asked.

Barb didn't know what to say. She studied her feet for a second, then regarded the house again. "I mean, you live in a nice house and drive that sports car. What do you need a truck like that for?"

"You don't want the money?"

"Yes, we want the money," Travis said, trying to silence Barb with a look.

"I need the truck for hauling stuff," Daniel said. "You know like groceries and—" he looked to Sarah for help.

"Books," Sarah said.

"Books. Things like that." Daniel held Barb's eyes until she looked away. He watched Travis sign his name to the the back of the title and hand it to him and as he took it, he said, "I was just lucky enough to find a truck with the black-power flag already on it."

"What?" Travis screwed up his face, trying to understand.

"The black-power flag on the window. You mean, you didn't know?"

Travis and Barb looked at each other.

"Well, anyway," Daniel said, "I'm glad we could do business." He turned to Sarah. "Let me take you for a ride in my new truck." He and Sarah walked across the yard, got into the pickup, and waved to Travis and Barb who were still standing in Daniel's yard as they drove away.

Sarah was on the verge of hysterics by the time they were out of sight. "That was beautiful," she said.

"No," Daniel said, softly. "That was true."

◆

Over the next weeks, sightings of Daniel and his truck proved problematic for some. He was accosted by two big white men in a '72 Monte Carlo in the parking lot of a 7-Eleven on Two Notch Road.

"What are you doing with that on your truck, boy?" the bigger of the two asked.

"Flying it proudly," Daniel said, noticing the rebel front plate on the Chevrolet. "Just like you, brothers."

The confused second man took a step toward Daniel. "What did you call us?"

"Brothers."

The second man pushed Daniel in the chest with two extended fists, but not terribly hard.

"I don't want any trouble," Daniel told them.

Then a Volkswagen with four black teenagers parked in the slot beside Daniel's truck and they jumped out, staring and looking serious. "What's going on?" the driver and largest of the teenagers asked.

"They were admiring our flag," Daniel said, pointing to his truck.

The teenagers were confused.

"We fly the flag proudly, don't we, young brothers?" Daniel gave a bent-arm, black-power, closed-fist salute. "Don't we?" he repeated. "Don't we?"

"Yeah," the young men said.

The white men had backed away to their car. They slipped into it and drove away.

Daniel looked at the teenagers and, with as serious a face as he could manage, he said, "Get a flag and fly it proudly."

◆

At a gas station, a lawyer named Ahmad Wilson stood filling the tank of his BMW and staring at the back window of Daniel's truck. He then looked at Daniel. "Your truck?" he asked.

Daniel stopped cleaning the windshield and nodded.

Wilson didn't ask a question, just pointed at the rear window of Daniel's pickup.

"Power to the people," Daniel said and laughed.

◆

Daniel played "Dixie" in another bar in town, this time with a R&B dance band at a banquet of the black medical association. The strange looks and expressions of outrage changed to bemused laughter and finally to open joking and acceptance as the song was played fast enough for dancing. Then the song was sung, slowly, to the profound surprise of those singing the song. *I wish I was in the land of cotton, old times there are not forgotten . . . Look away, look away, look away . . .*

◆

Soon, there were several, then many cars and trucks in Columbia, South Carolina, sporting Confederate flags and being driven by black people. Black businessmen and ministers wore rebel-flag buttons on their lapels and clips on their ties. The marching band of South Carolina State College, a predominantly black land-grant institution in Orangeburg, paraded with the flag during homecoming. Black people all over the state flew the Confederate flag. The symbol began to disappear from the fronts of big rigs and the back windows of jacked-up four-wheelers. And after the emblem was used to dress the yards and mark picnic sites of black family reunions the following Fourth of July, the piece of cloth was quietly dismissed from its station with the U.S. and State flags atop the State Capitol. There was no ceremony, no notice. One day, it was not there.

*Look away, look away, look away . . .*

# Warm and Nicely Buried

◆

Warren Fragua was always eating piñon nuts and this night was no different. You could always find him because of his trail of shells. Lem Becker liked Fragua because he knew more about fly-fishing than anyone he had ever met. Lem wished it were spring and that the two of them were down at the confluence of the Rio Grande and the Red River.

"You know these people well, Warren?" Lem asked, pulling out onto the main highway. The road surface was slick, the traffic melting the snow and the wind freezing the water.

"I arrested José when he was sixteen for stealing a car. I've checked on him from time to time since then. Not really a good kid, but I didn't think he was too bad. He and his old man fought like crazy, but that's not strange."

"Been in any trouble since the car theft?"

"Not caught for anything. I can't imagine him in anything big-time though. What the hell's big around here anyway?" Fragua cracked a piñon with his teeth. "Sheriff doesn't think it was an accident. If that's true, then something big got those guys killed."

Lem turned the defroster on high and leaned forward, wiped the inside of the windshield with his glove.

"That just makes it worse," Fragua said.

"That's what I hear."

"You been tying any?"

"Bunch of nymphs," Lem said. "Some zug-bugs, Tellicos, some early brown stoneflies. And some grasshoppers and little black beetles. You?"

"I've been tying a bunch of parachute Royal Coachmen. They're fun to tie. Fall to the water real nice, too."

They were silent for a while and Lem's mind returned to the sour business at hand. "Don't you hate telling people stuff like this?"

Fragua looked through the windshield as if studying something. "I'd like to say it's just part of the job. But it's always terrible."

"What were they doing out there?" Lem asked Fragua and himself.

"We'll know more when the State Police report comes in. Who knows, maybe the Marotta kid got picked up hitchhiking, and they stayed out there to smoke some dope." Fragua offered Lem some nuts.

"Yeah, right."

"Maybe they were transported there by aliens."

"That's more likely."

"Turn here," Fragua said. "They live down across the creek."

Lem followed Fragua's directions and they found the house after driving past it twice because of the snow. They walked up onto the porch and stomped

the snow off their boots while they waited for someone to answer. A young woman opened the chained
door, saw the uniformed men, and closed it. The door
was opened again by an older woman.

"Mr. Fragua," the woman said, half smiling, seeming to see something in the officer's face and falling
back a tiny step. "We haven't seen you for a long time."
She moved back to let them into the house.

"I know," Fragua said. "I've been really busy, as I'm
sure you've been."

"Yes, yes, very busy." She closed the door. "Especially with the church."

"This is Officer Becker."

Mrs. Marotta smiled at Lem, then turned her attention again to Fragua. "What is wrong?"

"Where is Mr. Marotta?"

"He's at my mother's house. I just talked to him a
couple of minutes ago."

"It's José," Fragua said.

Mrs. Marotta sat on the sofa. Lem looked up to
see the young woman in the doorway of the kitchen.
Fragua sat down beside the boy's mother.

"I called the police this morning because he didn't
come home for two nights. He's never been gone for
two nights," Mrs. Marotta said. "You have him in jail?"
She shook her head. "What has he done now?"

Fragua rubbed his temple, then took the woman's
hand. The young woman in the kitchen doorway
gasped audibly and disappeared. "I'm sorry, Mrs.
Marotta, but there's been an accident."

*"Dios mio,"* the woman said and tears were already finding her cheeks.

"José is dead."

The woman crumpled into Fragua's arms, sobbing. Sobbing came from the kitchen. Here, someone had had time to consider how they were going to break the worst of news and the result was no different than when he had done it clumsily.

A man came in through the back door and entered the living room through the kitchen. He was very confused, on the verge of being angry, beginning to pace. *"Que le ocurre?"* the man asked his wife.

The old woman just sobbed more.

Fragua stood and took the man's hand. "José is dead, Mr. Marotta."

The man's face went blank. He went to an overstuffed chair and sat, looking straight ahead.

Lem knew that they weren't going to get anywhere asking questions tonight. They'd have to come back tomorrow.

"What happened?" Mr. Marotta asked.

"As far as we can tell," Fragua said, "José was with three other men in a van and they were trying to keep warm with a stove and they smothered themselves."

The old woman howled.

Mr. Marotta went to his wife and held her. The young woman ran in from the kitchen and sat on the sofa, too, pressing up against her father.

Fragua looked at Lem who nodded. "We'll talk again in the morning. Officer Becker and I have some questions we need to ask."

The deputies left.

Lem and Fragua didn't speak on their way back to the station. Lem just let the other man out.

Lem walked into his house and looked at his walls, funky furniture, and unwashed dishes in the sink and breathed easier. He peeled off his hat and coat, went to the gas heater and turned it to high. His shoes off, he slipped into the moose-hide moccasins his mother had given him last Christmas. He looked at the collection of feathers and patches of hair and spools of thread on his desk.

He went to the kitchen, poured himself a tall glass of orange juice, then returned to sit behind the vise clamped to his desktop. He secured a size 10 hook and imagined a trout on the Henry's Fork River in Idaho rising for the Green Drake he was about to tie. He recalled watching his father spending the cold winter nights reading and tying flies for the next season. Lem finally asked his father to teach him to tie, not because he wanted to catch fish so much, but because he thought the flies were beautiful. He was ten at the time and he could still remember watching his first colorful streamer develop in the vise in front of him, and the way it felt to trim the deer hair on his first grasshopper, the pieces of feathers floating, how much fun it was to dub the muskrat fur onto the thread with his thumb and index finger. He laughed at himself. He hadn't even put the first winds of thread on the hook and he was already feeling better.

As he dubbed a mixture of yellow rabbit and tan-red

fox fur onto the olive thread he recalled his father.
He no longer felt sad when he thought of him. In
fact, thinking of him made Lem relax. They had been
close, for some reason they never had the conflicts his
friends did with their fathers. He wondered if his pres-
ent profession would have caused a problem between
them. He wondered himself why he did it. Somehow
he felt out of touch with his time; that was how he put
it. He didn't feel like people his age. He wanted to be
a part of another generation. He shook his head now
as he played it over in his brain. He wasn't like a lot
of people who became policemen, didn't want to be
like them, but then most of the lawmen in those parts
weren't like that, not *tough*, not *hard*, but doing a job
that made them feel pretty good. He worked the griz-
zly hackle around the body and turned his mind again
to trout.

The morning that came was as quiet as sleep, the layer
of snow smothering the sounds of daybreak. He sat now
at the edge of his mattress, his brain still tethered to
the remnants of a dream. He was chasing another man
on a dirt bike. It was a kind of game, he thought, since
they were both laughing. They were riding over rough
terrain, bouncing high and sliding, but there were
buildings there. Finally, Lem stopped and the other
man came back to him and together they observed
Lem's badly warped front wheel. It seemed a common
thing, no surprise to either of them, and so Lem lifted
the bike and carried it. The logic of the dream began to
disintegrate as his eyes opened more fully.

He rubbed the back of his neck and looked out the window at the foot of snow. The sky was clear of any promise of more bad weather, a brilliant cobalt blue that lifted his spirits and also told him that the hour was late. He found his watch on the stand by his bed. It was nearly eight.

Still, he took his time showering, enjoying the steaming spray. There were a lot of things wrong with his small house, but the shower was not one of them. The water was good and hot and the pressure was strong, like in some gym locker rooms, the droplets of water seeming to pierce the skin like tiny darts. He dried off, got dressed, and went into the kitchen where he fried himself some bacon and a couple of eggs. He appreciated these early hours alone, wanted them to last, but they wouldn't, they couldn't. When he was finished eating, he readied himself for the cold and went out to free his car from the snow.

As he cleared the ice from the windshield he thought of his business that morning. He had to go question the Marottas and go through the kid's room. That wouldn't be pleasant, but at least Warren Fragua would be with him.

The incompetent highway crews had done a good job of transforming the hazardous roads into deadly sheets of ice. They had also done a beautiful job of dumping endless strands of salt and sand down along the center line where no one's tires would ever touch it. He parked in front of the station and entered just behind Fragua.

Once inside he was shoulder to shoulder with Fragua, staring at the chubby finger Sheriff Bucky Paz was pointing at them. "I want the two of you to go to Fonda's Funeral Home right now."

"What's the problem?"

"Somebody broke in there last night and walked away with José Marotta."

"Stole his body?" Fragua said.

"Apparently. All I know is Fonda got there this morning and the boy was gone. By the way, that truck last night was stolen from Taos, reported five days ago. Now, go."

Lem drove. The acquisition of so many dead bodies was unusual for the Plata Sheriff's Department and the only place to put them was the same place a single body would have been put, Fonda's Funeral Home. From there the bodies were to go to the forensic pathologist in Santa Fe for autopsies.

"I'll bet Fonda just misplaced him," Fragua said.

"Why would anyone take a dead body?" Lem wondered aloud. "Maybe the kid swallowed a bunch of dope in balloons and the bad guys want it back."

"You've been watching television again. I told you, just tie every night and your mind won't get polluted."

"You watch television all the time," Lem said.

"So, I ought to know, right?"

Lem slammed on the brakes to avoid hitting a pickup that skidded through a stop sign.

Fragua braced himself with a hand against the dash. "Don't think about it. Let it happen. That's what my daughter says. 'Let it happen.' And I tell her she better not let *it* happen. You know what I mean."

Lem smiled.

"It's like tying flies," the Indian said.

"Everything for you is like tying flies."

"True. But listen. You've got to tie things down in the right order or it won't work. You can't go tying down the tinsel after the body or tie the tail on last and expect it to look right. Everything works in the same way, one step at a time, but the right step."

"I never knew you were such a philosopher."

Fonda was a square man, not very tall, but wide-shouldered with large features, huge eyes and nose, and big hands and, like so many morticians, Lem thought, drained of all blood and body heat. He was mad, but like the funeral director he was, he wasn't unsettled. "What can I tell you?" he said. "I came in this morning and the boy was gone."

"Is there any sign of forced entry?" Lem asked, following Fonda into the back room with three tables with bodies and one without.

"Forced entry?" the man said, almost a giggle in his voice. "It's a robbery, not a rape." He laughed.

Lem sighed and caught his eyes. "That's not funny," Lem said.

"Excuse me," Fonda said sarcastically.

"Forced entry?"

"I don't know," Fonda said. "This place has a hundred windows. This is a funeral home. I never expected break-ins. All I know is that he didn't get up and walk away.

"So, get your clues and get out. It's bad for business to have you seen here."

"How do you figure that?" Fragua asked.

"Cops are bad for any business," Fonda said. "Unless you own a doughnut shop." He laughed again.

Lem watched as Fragua walked past the bodies to the empty table. "Mr. Fonda, you're the only undertaker in this town. I doubt our presence will affect your good work."

"Just do what you have to do and get out." He started out of the room.

"Was anybody working here last night?" Fragua asked.

Exasperated, Fonda answered, "No."

"Emilio still work for you?" Lem asked. "What's his last name?"

"Vilas. And yes, he still works for me."

"When will he be in?" Lem didn't like being in the room with the dead and he was beginning to get jumpy. He tried to breathe slowly and deeply.

"He's not coming in today. I usually call him when I need him. Now, if that's all?" He turned and walked through the doorway and out of sight.

"Man, he's a real charmer, isn't he?" Lem said.

Fragua ran his finger along the edge of the table. "Well, do we look at the 'hundred' windows?"

"If it's that easy to get in, why bother? They probably came in through the front door." Lem looked around the room, at the covered forms and, aside from the obvious, something wasn't right.

"You know they say Fonda's funny," Fragua said in a hushed voice.

"You mean funny—ha-ha or funny—peculiar?"

"You never heard anybody say, 'Fonda's fonda boys?'"

"I never heard that," Lem said, checking the doorway, "but I heard 'Fonda dead bodies.'" Lem felt badly for talking about the man. "You know, if you're the only undertaker in town, people are bound to talk and make up stuff." Lem turned his attention back to the empty table. "José didn't get up and walk out. Think we should get the kit and dust for prints?"

"I don't think we're going to find anything."

"Yeah, I agree." Lem blew out a breath, almost a whistle. "We've got to tell the boy's parents."

"Shit."

"This sucks," Lem said, rubbing his forehead.

"You thought she freaked out last night," Fragua said. "You wait until that good Catholic woman finds out her boy's not going to get a Christian burial. You wait until she finds out that some devils have stolen him."

They didn't tell Fonda they were leaving.

To keep his mind from the unpleasant business of talking with the Marottas and later having to fill out the case reports that he had let pile up the last few days, Lem imagined the life of Armand Fonda. He knew where the man lived, in a very nice and sprawling adobe north of town, a Cyclone fence looking out of place surrounding it. He remembered another musing of his father, that it seemed Cyclone fences did little to keep out cyclones. He laughed in his head, thinking that Fonda's fence worked. No cyclone had touched his house since he put up the barrier. Fonda got up, he thought, had a nice grapefruit half with one of those special spoons that Lem's mother owned but never used; it sat in her drawer full of odd and useless gadgets, like the plastic box that shaped boiled eggs into cubes. Fonda talked to his little dog, a Pekingese or something, cooed to it like it was his little boy. Then he imagined that the man had all sorts of funereal trade journals around, about caskets and embalming, *Mortician's Monthly* and maybe *Fluid Facts*. Death was a strange thing to choose to be around.

Lem shook his head clear and viewed the neighborhood of the Marottas in the daylight. Small poorly maintained adobes stood in a row, awkward wood-framed additions poking out of most, testimony to their disregard for family planning. Sheep and chickens wandered yards and an occasional horse stood under a rough shed. The other side of the road was open, an arroyo splitting it about thirty yards in. There was a wreath on the front door of the Marotta house. The snow made it all so peaceful, so soft, gentle, and so, sadder.

Fragua knocked. Mrs. Marotta came to the door, her eyes red from crying and lack of sleep, but less confused after a night of praying. She was expecting the visit from the police so she was not thrown by it. She let them into the living room and asked them to sit, offered them coffee, which they declined.

Fragua sat, but Lem wandered off to stand by the window and look out at the field across the road and the hills rising beyond it.

"Please," Fragua said, gesturing that the woman sit by him on the sofa.

Mrs. Marotta looked even smaller today, Lem thought, viewing her from behind, her narrow shoulders slumping toward her heart.

"Mrs. Marotta, José is gone."

The woman took Fragua's hand and patted it as if consoling him. "Yes, my son is dead." She assured him that her feet were planted firmly on real ground.

"Mrs. Marotta, I don't know how to tell you this. I'm really sorry." These words were coming harder than the ones last night delivering news of the boy's death. "Someone broke into Fonda's Funeral Home last night and they took José's body."

The woman's head turned so that she could take the deputy in fully. Then she shook her head. She looked as if she just couldn't make the words have meaning.

"José is gone. His body was stolen and we don't know where it is."

The woman crumpled, fainted, fell over away from Fragua onto the sofa as if she'd been shot.

"Christ!" Lem said.

The daughter came running from another room and let out a short scream. Fragua lifted the woman's head in his hands, stroked dark hair from her face.

Lem went to the phone to dial the paramedics. "Mama, mama," the girl pleaded with her mother to regain consciousness. Fragua told the girl to go get a glass of water.

Lem put down the phone. "They're on their way. Is she all right?"

"I think so. She's breathing okay."

The girl came back with the water and a damp rag. Fragua took the rag and let her hold the glass while he wiped the woman's face. Lem watched the girl tremble as she watched the still and silenced face of her mother. This was why he worked this job, to see this, to learn something about life, but he had learned nothing, was learning nothing. Life was empty here in this house where this woman kept things so clean, so tidy, and her god was not here for her, he believed this. Then on the wall he saw it. He hadn't noticed it last night, but there it was, a crucifix affixed to the plaster and a bare-chested Jesus Christ wrapped in a skirt. These people were Penitentes. The Penitentes were a secret order of Catholics who practiced rather severe bodily penance and recondite burials of their dead. Not having a body to put into the earth was going to be a very big deal for the Marottas. Lem felt close to crying as he watched the old woman begin to come around. He heard the paramedics' truck squeal to a halt outside. He went to the door and let them in with a blast of cold air that he was certain would aid in the woman's revival. Fragua stood away and let the medics work.

Lem went to the girl. "Are you okay?"

She nodded.

He pulled strands of her long dark hair from her face. "My name is Lem. What's yours?"

"Rosa."

"Rosa, everything's going to be all right." He put his arm around her and gave her a hug. "Will you show me which room is your brother's?"

She nodded and walked down the hall. Lem and Fragua followed. She stood away from the door. Fragua entered while Lem bent to address the girl. "Your mother's probably going to need you out there."

"I'll start looking over here," Fragua said as Lem entered. He was sitting on the unmade bed, opening the drawer of the nightstand.

Lem went to the dresser by the window. "These people are Penitentes," he reported.

Fragua looked at him. "That's real tough."

They went back to their searching. Lem had worked his way to the bottom drawer of the beat-up dresser, peeling past the boy's sweaters and T-shirts, when Fragua said, "Oh my god." He turned to see the Indian holding a blue notebook in his lap. "Look at this."

Lem looked on from beside him. The pages were filled with drawings of pentagram-marked monsters and horned devils and bloody, ripped-up bodies, all done in black ink, each figure underscored by a rough rust-colored streak. "Do you suppose that's blood?" Lem asked.

Fragua swallowed hard. "I think it is. It's the same all the way through."

"You know teenagers draw shit like that all the time. I mean, that's nothing unusual," Lem said.

"I suppose."

"Where did you find that?" Lem asked.

"Top shelf, closet."

Lem went to the closet and pulled a shoe box down from the same shelf, uncovered it. "Howdy, boys." He tilted the container toward Fragua so he could have a look at the stack of bills. Lem counted them out. "Two hundred sixty-three dollars and this little stash here." He held up the small vial of white powder to the light through the window. He unscrewed the cap, dipped his finger, took a taste. "Yep." He sighed. "And this. What do you think it is?"

Fragua looked at the plastic bag that Lem dangled in his face. "Looks like some little animal's heart."

"That's what it looks like to me, too. What was this kid? A devil worshipper or something?" He sat on the bed next to his partner. "Listen, I'm just a dumb cowboy. This is too much for me."

"And I just want to be on a stream somewhere."

"Are you scared?"

"You bet."

Lem heard crying on the other side of the door. He opened the door and startled Rosa Marotta. He stepped into the hallway with her and closed the door so she wouldn't see any of the things they had found. In the living room he could see the paramedics still tending to the mother.

"It's okay, Rosa," he said, touching her hair. "We really want to help. Will you help, too?"

The girl looked at him.

"Was your brother acting strange?"

She nodded.

"How so?"

She sucked in her sobbing. "He would sing in his room, strange things I didn't understand." She looked to see that her mother was still on the sofa. "The way he looked at me sometimes scared me."

"Did he have any friends?"

"A guy named Emilio. They spent a lot of time together."

"You know his last name?"

Rosa shook her head, then straightened at the sound of the paramedics leaving.

"Is his name Vilas?" Lem asked quickly.

Rosa shrugged, looking toward the living room.

"Thank you, Rosa."

Fragua came out of the bedroom in time to see Rosa walking toward her mother. He was carrying the notebook and the shoe box and he put them into Lem's hands. "I'll talk to Mrs. Marotta and you get these outside."

Lem nodded and walked behind him to the living room.

Mrs. Marotta was standing, hugging her daughter. Fragua went to her and put his hand on her back. "Are you all right now, Mrs. Marotta?" he asked.

She nodded. She was still crying a little.

Fragua continued to console her with phrases that to Lem grew more and more empty for their repetition. Lem said nothing to her and walked out to stand beneath a sky that had again turned gray. He stood by the car and waited for the other officer. He looked at the field across the road. To live with such beauty, he thought. You really didn't need money if you could see land like this, just open your door and have it be there. About fifty yards away he spotted a coyote lurking in the brush.

"Are you ready to go?" Fragua asked from behind him, waking him.

They got into the car. "Rosa told me that José spent a lot of time with somebody named Emilio."

Lem finished turning the car around in the narrow road. "That would be convenient, wouldn't it? Seems likely, too. I tell you what, you go talk to Mr. Marotta and I'll go track down Emilio."

Lem drove to the little duplex on Carson Road that was supposed to be the home of Emilio Vilas, but no one answered his knock. He knocked on the door of the other unit and a robed, middle-aged woman with bright red hair responded, rubbing her eyes, annoyed.

"I'm looking for Emilio Vilas," Lem said.

"Well, he doesn't live *here*," she said.

"Sorry to disturb you, ma'am. Do you know Emilio?"

"He lives next door, but I don't know him. I've got enough trouble."

"Trouble?"

She looked at the deputy as if he were stupid. "Men are trouble."

"So, you wouldn't have any idea where he is."

"No, I wouldn't. Try a bar. He's a damn alcoholic."

"Thank you, ma'am."

She didn't say anything, just slammed her door.

Lem decided to take the woman's advice and check the nearby bars. He drove by one, kicking himself because he hadn't thought to ask what Emilio's car looked like. He entered three taverns and asked if anyone had seen the kid. He received little cooperation. Luckily, he had a vague memory of Emilio's face and in the third dive he saw him. Emilio panicked and made a dash for the back door. Lem gave chase, leaping over a chair, squeezing through stacked crates in front of the rear exit to get outside only to see Emilio's heels and elbows speeding down the alley. The kid hit a patch of ice and slid into several garbage cans, screamed, and grabbed his leg. He looked back at the deputy trotting toward him, but didn't get up.

Lem stood over the young man. "How you doing?" He thought it was a funny thing to say.

Emilio just looked at him.

"Broken?"

"No, I just twisted it. What you want with me, man?"

Lem sat, straddling an upset garbage can. "You hear about José?"

"Yeah, he's dead. What's that got to do with me?"

"You were pals, right?"

"Yeah, I guess." He continued to rub his leg.

A mouse or a small rat bolted from the garbage and across Lem's feet and he let loose with a short scream. So much for the macho front. He looked up and down the cold, empty alley. "What do you know about José's body?"

"I don't know nothing about his body. What do you mean, 'what do I know about his body?'"

"His body's gone, stolen right out of the funeral home."

"Yeah, so?"

"You work there, don't you?"

"Sure, but, man, I didn't have nothing to do with José's body."

"So, you knew about it?"

"Of course I knew about it. I work there." He stopped rubbing his leg and looked toward where the alley opened onto Norte Drive.

"Who are you looking for?"

"Nobody."

"Do you have any idea how they got into Fonda's?"

Emilio shook his head.

"Can you walk?"

Emilio pulled himself up and tested his leg, nodded.

"Come on, let me buy you a cup of coffee," Lem said.

"I need to be going." He tossed another quick glance toward Norte.

"No, I really want to buy you a cup of coffee." Lem looked at his eyes. "It's the least I can do." He stood and righted the can, put the lid on it. "Come on." He supported the man.

Emilio snatched his arm free of the deputy's help. Lem walked him back into the tavern where they sat in a dimly lit booth. He called for the bartender to bring them a couple cups of coffee.

"So, what kind of stuff was José into?" Lem asked.

"How would I know?"

The bartender brought the coffee and gave Emilio a hard stare.

"What's his problem?" Emilio asked, watching the man return to the bar.

"Cops are bad for business." Lem blew at his coffee. "Tell me about José. Tell me about his cocaine deal."

"What deal? José tooted a little now and then. Big fucking deal."

"Listen, kid, you can cut the tough stuff. I don't want to fight with you. I just want to find José so his mama can put him in the ground and feel okay. Hear what I'm saying?"

"José didn't have no deal."

"All right. What about the devil shit he was into?"

Emilio shook his head nervously. "I don't know what you're talking about."

"The guy kept a rat's heart in a Baggie. He was into something funny. Listen, you were his friend, so tell me what you know."

"We were friends. We scored some dope together, got high, got drunk, but I don't know what he was into, man. Honest. He was acting real strange the last few months. I really didn't see him that much."

Lem nodded, starting to believe him. "What do you think of your boss?"

"Mr. Fonda? He's weird as shit, but he's okay. You don't have to worry about him. Listen, José's mother is going to be all right. Don't sweat it. She's not . . . you know what I mean?"

Everything suddenly fell into place. The Marottas

were not about to let some state pathologist desecrate the body of their son. "I know what you mean," Lem said. "Fonda's weird?"

"The way he acts. I don't know. He's cold like he's dead or something." Emilio hadn't touched his coffee. Now, he sat looking down at the cup.

"You don't drink coffee?"

"Don't need it."

"What was José doing up on Plata Ridge?"

"I don't know."

"If he wasn't hanging out with you, then who was he hanging out with? Do you know who they were?"

"I don't know. I don't know nothing. I didn't see him a lot lately, okay?"

"Okay." Lem looked at Emilio over the rim of his cup as he finished his coffee. "If you think of anything, give me a call."

Emilio nodded.

Fragua was eating piñon nuts like crazy, cracking and chewing, and brushing the spent shells off his lap onto the floor of Lem's truck. Lem looked at him and then at the mess.

"You're going to clean that up, aren't you?" Lem asked with a raised eyebrow.

"Clean what up?"

"The shells."

"This is natural waste, bio-stuff. No need to clean these up. They'll break down naturally and contribute to the ecosystem, which is your car." Fragua laughed and sucked at some food that had become caught between his teeth. He looked out the window and yawned. "I love the early morning."

"Does Mary like to get up early, too?"

"Can't stand it. She's a night person. Stays up all hours puttering around the house and watching television. She gets up just after me, though. I don't know how she does it. She must get four hours of sleep, five tops."

"I need eight," Lem said.

"Me, too." Fragua studied Lem for a moment. "You want to talk about yesterday?"

"Not really. I do have something to tell you. I talked to Emilio last night."

"Yeah?"

"I found out something about José Marotta's body."

"Don't tell me," Fragua said. "If you know, that's fine and let's keep it that way."

"You knew," Lem said.

Fragua looked out the passenger-side window.

"How'd you know?"

"I'm not sure. I guess the Marottas didn't convince me. Mr. Marotta was too upset and Mrs. Marotta wasn't upset enough. She didn't really faint. Hell, I don't know, but I knew they had him."

"Enough said on the matter."

Lem pulled off the highway and onto the dirt road that led to Garapata Mesa. His truck bounced wildly along the wagon-rutted lane even though he was driving slowly.

# Afraid of the Dark

◆

An unusual morning rain had come through and left the ground just barely wet. Austin cantered around the arena and was pleased to not breathe in the familiar dust. He ran along the north rail and practiced rollbacks. His mule was getting the hang of it, but still he was a mule and wanted to think about everything before he did it. Austin considered the fact that he had to be smarter than his animal. Apparently, spending most of the hours of most of his days working his equine friends hadn't made him that smart. It had made him broke and divorced, but not smart. Sarah said as she left, "You go out on trails all right, but what you really love is riding around in circles." She said that and drove away in a Chevy with a weak battery to the house of another man.

"Damn if that ain't the horsiest-looking mule I ever saw," Dwight Twins said from the gate. He had one of his small, sneakered feet set up on the bottom rail.

Austin turned the mule and let him walk toward the man. "How long have you been there?"

"Couple minutes. Long enough to pronounce that

the fastest mule in the county. Does he go where you want him to?"

"On occasion." Austin leaned forward to rub the animal's big red neck. "I'm thinking of trying him at steer wrestling in the little rodeo."

"I thought he was scared of cows."

"It's true he doesn't like them that much, but he's not afraid of them anymore."

"Well, good luck." Dwight spat onto the ground, his way of indicating his own sarcasm.

"I was wondering if you'd come be my hazer."

"Can't. Gotta drive up to Pueblo and pick up a horse for Delores Rainey. Get Dougie to do it for you."

Austin laughed. "Dougie couldn't haze a steer straight if he ran a cable through his mouth and out his ass."

"Anyway," Dwight said, "you should ride up to Colorado with me instead of killing yourself down here. You don't need no rodeo to prove that mule."

"Maybe you're right."

"Delores wants me to pick up her little brother in Trinidad on the way back."

"I didn't know she had a brother."

"Me neither. I guess he's a fuckup."

"There're a few of those around." Austin swung his right leg over the mule's neck and slid off the saddle.

"So, what do you say? Pass up a mouth full of dirt and a broken collar bone for a long boring drive and stale, predictable conversation?"

"When you put it that way." Austin loosened the

girth and scratched the mule's belly. "Delores must be eighty. How old is this little brother?"

"I don't know. Seventy? I don't know. His name is Myron, but she calls him Yeahbutt."

Austin looked at Dwight.

"She told me he always has to have the last word, so he's always saying, 'Yeah, but.'"

"Cute. So, what's Yeahbutt doing in Trinidad?"

"Don't know. Delores gave me the address and an extra fifty. That's all I need."

"Okay, I'll go."

"Pick you up at five."

"Make it five-fifteen so I can get the animals fed."

Dwight Twins was famous for being late except for mornings when he was early. He showed up at 4:00 and Austin was just struggling into consciousness.

"Am I early?" Dwight asked.

"Hell yeah, you're early." Austin rubbed his eyes. "It's four o'clock, man. Jesus, what do you do? Drive around waking up roosters?"

"Sorry."

"Well, make some coffee while I get dressed."

"It's going to rain later on," Dwight said. "Weather Wally predicted it on the radio."

Austin closed the bathroom door and leaned on the sink, looked at his face in the mirror. "Weather Wally can't predict daybreak."

Austin got dressed, sipped from a mug of coffee, then put it down. "I'll go feed the animals and we can grab a bite on the road."

"Sounds like a plan."

"Well, it ain't."

"You're not pretty in the morning, are you?"

Austin climbed into the passenger seat of Dwight's truck and stopped him before he was out of the yard. "What did you do? Did you take all the stuffing out of this seat?"

"Basically. I put it on this side because the bumps hurt my behind."

"I can't ride all the way to Pueblo on this buck-board bench." Austin looked out the window at the moon. "Back this thing up. Let's put the trailer on my truck and I'll drive."

"Okay, but I'm paying for the gas."

"You're damn right you're paying for the gas."

They hitched the trailer to Austin's pickup and left at first light. Dwight laughed to himself. "You know why cowboys all have the same-sized balls?"

"No, why?"

"So they can pull each other's trailers. That's an old one, but I love it."

"What did you say that made me say yes to going with you?" Austin asked.

Dwight shrugged.

On the interstate, Dwight said, "I don't know if it matters much to you, but I don't think Sarah should have left."

Austin sighed agreement.

"I was surprised when she picked up the way she did. I mean, just out of the blue like that. I suppose you were in a better place to see it coming. For another man."

"Yeah."

"Must have hurt like hell. She's a damn beautiful woman."

"Dwight," Austin said, "you want to shut the hell up?"

"Sure thing."

Austin considered his soon-to-be-ex-wife. It had hurt like hell. And it had probably been all his fault, but recognizing that so late wasn't going to help and sure didn't ease the pain. He looked over at Dwight and the older man smiled at him.

"You ever been dumped?" Austin asked.

"Hell, who hasn't?" Dwight said. He rolled his window down another inch.

"This is my first time."

'Scary, ain't it?"

Austin turned his attention back to the highway.

Four hours later they were ouside Pueblo picking up Delores's horse. He was a beautiful black and white paint with wild eyes and a piebald nose. He pranced around the corral and Austin noticed that he searched for balance here and there with his left hind leg. He and Dwight were standing there with the former owner.

"Did Delores get a vet check on this guy?" Austin asked.

Dwight didn't know.

The other man, named Hicks, said, "She came up and looked him over."

"He acts like he's got the wobbles. Look at how he moves in his back end." The horse was trotting away from them. "He's all loose like he's crazy in the caboose."

"Delores saw him move," Hicks said.

"All I know is I'm supposed to pick him up and deliver him," Dwight said.

"Why isn't he cut?" Austin asked.

"Somebody might want to breed him," Hicks said.

"Let it go, Austin," Dwight said.

Austin thought better of saying any more. It wasn't his deal. He'd seen horse traders like this man before and if Delores didn't care, he sure as hell wasn't going to.

Hicks twisted up his face as if thinking. "Austin. You that guy whose wife left for that goat roper?"

"Let's get this horse loaded," Austin said.

"Well, you boys ought to get home before dark, easy," Hicks said as the gate of the trailer closed against the horse's rump.

"We got to make a stop in Trinidad," Dwight said.

"How long a stop?" Hicks asked.

Austin thought the question was odd. He latched the door and stepped over to the man. "Why?" The thought flashed through his mind that maybe they were being set up for a hijacking.

"No reason. This horse does a little better when it's light out, is all. But he'll be fine. You fellers seem like you know what you're doing."

Right then, Austin was absolutely certain that

was not true. He and Dwight left with the horse, but Austin's stomach was already upset.

"Something bothering you?" Dwight asked.

"Just everything."

Austin and Dwight made it into Trinidad about lunch-time. They sat in a diner and downed some coffee and a couple of sandwiches before checking out the ad-dress Delores had given Dwight. Austin asked direc-tions a couple times and they found the street, then the house, a run-down aluminum-sided affair with a shake roof and an ancient Doberman on the porch. The dog lifted his head, then let it fall again. Dwight knocked. Again.

"It's the right number," Austin said, looking at the digits arranged vertically in front of him.

As they were stepping off the porch, the door opened.

"What do you want?" a fat woman asked. She was rubbing sleep from her eyes. Her giant T-shirt came to the middle of her thighs and giant, wide-legged jeans covered her the rest of the way to the floor.

"Is Myron Rainey here?" Dwight asked.

"No, he ain't here. Who are you?"

"His sister asked me to give him a ride down to Cimarron. You know where I can find him?"

"Try a bar."

"Any bar in particular?" Dwight asked.

"One that got booze in it." And with that she closed the door.

"Nothing's easy," Austin said as they walked back

to the truck. Austin stopped at the trailer and stroked
the tip of the horse's nose. "He's a nice animal. I
wouldn't ride him for a million dollars, but he seems
sweet."

"Well, let's hit a couple of taverns," Dwight said,
getting into the cab. When Austin was behind the
wheel, he added, "Just a couple. Hell, if he ain't at
hand, Delores will just have to live with it."

It was a bright afternoon and Austin felt strange walking into a tavern. He was blinded when he entered, and
he followed Dwight to the middle of the room. He let
his eyes adjust as he looked around. A couple of sad
rejects were slumped over the bar and a fiftyish woman
with with big, platinum hair was wiping out glasses.

They went to the woman and Dwight asked, "Do
you know a big guy named Myron Rainey?"

"Don't know nobody what's named Myron."

"They call him Yeahbutt."

"Oh, Yeahbutt." The woman smiled tenderly, while
shaking her head, as if considering a dead friend. "He
comes in here. Was in here last night. Ain't in here
now. He owe you money?"

"No ma'am," Dwight said. "You know where I might
find him?"

"No clue. I reckon he lives someplace, but I don't
know where."

"Thanks anyway."

The next place was a little better lighted and served
food as well as drinks and so there were more patrons
and they looked a little less pathetic. At the bar was

an enormous, hulking mound of human being and
Austin said, "I'll bet you that's him."

Dwight weaved through the tables, Austin behind
him. He tapped the big man on the shoulder. "Myron?"

The red, glazed eyes turned to them. The man
looked every bit of sixty-five, but was huge, three feet
wide and as tall as Dwight while still sitting.

"Are you Myron Rainey?" Dwight asked.

"Who the hell wants to know?" he slurred.

"Your sister asked me to give you a ride down to
New Mexico. My name is Dwight Twins. This here is
Austin."

"You think I give a flying fuck what your name is?
My sister, eh? You mean Delores?"

"Yeah. She told me you knew I was coming." Dwight
looked at Austin and then at the door.

"My sister sent *you* to pick *me* up?"

Dwight nodded.

"Ain't that some shit." Myron nudged the drunk
beside him with a elbow. "You hear that? She sent this
peewee to come pick me up." He looked at his empty
glass. "Well, okay." And he stood up. He was nearly
seven feet tall. Austin felt the front of his neck stretch.
"But I gotta hit your buddy."

"What?" Dwight asked.

"I'm gonna hit your pal here."

"Why? He didn't say a word."

"Yeah, but that's what bothers me." He swayed a
bit with the alcohol. He looked at Austin as if for the
first time. "Hey, you're black."

"I know." Austin studied his balled-up fist. "I would

prefer if you didn't hit me," Austin said, starting to fall back a step, plotting a path through the tables to daylight.

Myron showed a rotten tooth in the side of his smile. He then pulled his fist back and let go with a lumbering swing. Austin moved with the blow, catching just a bit of its sting, and remained standing. Chairs squawked as people made room.

"Yeahbutt!" the bartender shouted. "I told you about fighting in here." He picked up the phone. "Now I'm calling the sheriff."

Myron wasn't listening however. He had reloaded and was launching another fist. Austin stepped inside this time and latched onto the big man's torso. He had his arms and legs wrapped around Myron and was completely off the floor. Myron pounded his back.

"Get him off me," Myron slurred. "Off me."

"The sheriff is on his way, Yeahbutt."

Austin felt the man's body sagging and so he clamped down harder, squeezing for all he was worth. Dwight was dancing around them. "Dwight, what the hell are you doing?!" Austin shouted.

"He looks like he's about to go," Dwight said.

Then Myron was sinking to his knees. Austin relaxed his grip, found the floor with his feet, and stepped away. The big man fell like a tree onto his face.

The bartender leaned over the bar to look. "You boys need to get that mountain out of here before the sheriff comes. That son of a bitch will happily lock all three of you up."

"I didn't do anything," Austin said.

"Don't matter a mouse's tit to the sheriff."

"Shit, okay," Dwight said. "I say we leave him."

Austin considered Delores Rainey. She was a nasty old lady, but still, this was her brother. "Grab a leg." Dwight started to complain. "Shut up and grab his other leg."

They dragged Myron past people who had gone back to their eating and drinking, through the front door, and into the bright parking lot. They stopped, leaning over, hands on knees, panting.

"This guy weighs a ton," Dwight said.

Myron stirred, muttered, "Yeah, but."

"Come on, let's get him into the back of the truck," Austin said. They each got under an arm and pushed and hoisted and wished the man over the wall into the bed.

Dwight had his hat off and was fanning himself. "Have mercy," he said. "I feel like my chest is gonna pop."

"Don't have a heart attack on me now." Austin started around the truck. "Get in. We'll stop down the road a piece and give the horse some more hay."

In the truck, Dwight said, "You know, he's right. You are black."

"Funny man."

As they rolled away from the tavern, the sheriff's rig pulled in.

A couple of miles out of Trinidad, Austin pulled off the freeway into a rest area with, notably, "no facilities." They got out and looked down at Myron from either side of the bed. He was still out, though he had managed to shift his body into a more comfortable-looking position. He snorted and twitched.

"At least he ain't dead," Dwight said.

"I reckon," Austin said. He walked back to the trailer and pulled the pin out of the back door. "I'll walk this boy around a bit while you muck out."

"Fair enough," Dwight said.

Austin backed the horse out of the trailer and led him off the gravel and down a short dirt path, let him nibble at what little grass there was. He looked at his watch and saw that it was nearly five. With any luck they might still make Cimarron by nightfall. He walked the horse back to Dwight, who was putting away the silage fork. They loaded the horse and stepped toward the cab. They stopped at their doors and backed up to look into the bed. Myron was not there.

"Did you see him move?" Austin asked.

"Nope."

"Shit."

"I say leave him," Dwight said.

"We can't leave him out here. Something bad will happen. A bear will find him or something."

"That's the bear's problem," Dwight said. "Listen, you're the one he wants to hit."

Austin looked toward the highway, then over at the steep downward slope. "He can't have gone far."

"He won't be hard to spot anyway."

"You go that way," Austin pointed south to a thicket. "Maybe he had to pee." While Dwight walked off toward the trees, Austin moved to the slope and looked down at the trickle of a creek. He let his eyes follow the stream south a ways, then spotted Myron trying to pull himself up the opposite side of the arroyo. "Good god." Myron would frantically climb a couple of feet then slide down, his front and face now covered with dirt. Austin called for Dwight and started down.

Dwight made it to the drop-off and said, "Good god."

"This guy is more than just drunk!" Austin yelled back.

Myron finally rolled over on his back and stared at the sky, heaving great breaths that filled his huge torso like a balloon.

Austin sloshed through the stream to stand over the man. "What the hell are you on?"

"Everything," Myron said.

"Well, you need to give it up."

"Yeah, but it helps me cope."

Dwight caught up to Austin. "Is he dead?"

"Maybe," Myron said. The big man looked at Austin. "Your name Austin?"

"Yep."

"Your woman left you?"

Austin looked at Dwight. "What the hell is going on? This is starting to piss me off."

"So, a few people know your business. Big deal."

"That's easy for you to say, you ain't got any business." Austin looked back at the hill. "Myron, we can't drag you back up. Do you think you can walk?"

"I'll try." Myron was sounding a little more coherent.

Myron did try. He pushed and grabbed onto the

knotty, woody shrubs and pulled, Austin and Dwight behind him, shoving at his hind end. Then he would slip and and there was nothing either of the smaller men could do to stop him. Then they'd start over. By the time they reached the top, Austin's watch told him it was six o'clock and the light was already changing. All three were exhausted. Myron got up and began to pace in a circle.

"Look at him," Dwight said. "He's got sleeping sickness. I saw a wildebeest on television do the same thing."

"Let's get going." Austin got up and steered Myron to the truck. They put him in the cab next to the passenger-side window. The three were wedged in tightly, Myron barely fitting his knees under the glove box.

On a 6 percent downgrade, Myron sat up abruptly, said, "I gotta vomit," and proceeded to open the door. Dwight made some unintelligible noise of terror, while Austin applied the trailer brake, then the truck's brakes. He tried to keep the rig straight while he glanced over at Dwight, stretched to his limit across the big man's body. Dwight's leg came up and his boot nearly hit Austin in the head. He grabbed Dwight briefly by his belt, then put both hands back on the wheel. The door clicked shut again and Myron threw up down between the door and seat, then turned to put some on Dwight.

"Godalmighty," Dwight said.

Austin got the truck stopped and off on the shoulder. He just sat where he was behind the wheel and closed his eyes for a second. He looked up as Dwight kicked open the door, then pushed Myron out onto ground. Austin got out and came around, standing well clear of both men.

"Look at me," Dwight said.

"You're a mess." Then Austin regarded his truck.

Myron was on his hands and knees, throwing up again.

"You could have gotten us killed," Austin said.

"Yeah, but I was sick."

Dwight peeled off his shirt and stood with his arms held away from his body. "Smells like shit."

"I'll get the horse's water." Austin went to the trailer. It was sundown and the cars that were speeding by had on their headlights. The horse stirred a bit. "Hang on, fella, just another hour."

Austin took two towels and the bucket of water to the front of the truck. He grabbed his flashlight from the glove box and looked at the mess. He tossed one towel to Dwight, dipped the other into the water, then started to wipe up the vomit. The smell was awful and he knew that it would take weeks of wind to blow it out.

"We can't put him back in the truck," Dwight said. "He'll get us killed for sure."

"We'll throw him in the back," Austin said.

"This fool will decide he has to take a leak and step out."

Dwight was right. There was no argument in Austin.

"I guess we'll have to tie him up." He and Dwight stood silently for a spell considering the idea. "What else can we do?"

So, they tied Myron up, bound his feet and hands. The man was already falling asleep. Austin looked up at the moon. As they were getting into the cab, they heard a loud noise from the trailer.

"You hear that?" Dwight asked.

"I did."

There was the noise again. They walked back to the trailer. The horse kicked the wall once more. Then a bunch of times. The trailer rocked and the horse kicked more, reared up and slammed his head into the roof.

"Damn!" Dwight let out. "What do we do?"

The horse was freaking out, kicking and rearing and screaming. Austin walked to the back of the trailer and considered opening the door, but decided against it. This crazy horse might kill him, then run like a maniac down the freeway. "I don't know what to do."

"We got to do something."

Both men made soothing sounds that the horse ignored. Austin was still holding the flashlight and, curious to see if the animal had done himself any damage, turned it on and pointed the beam into the trailer. The light hit the horse's eyes and he calmed down.

"What'd you do?" Dwight asked.

"I don't know." Austin turned off the light and the horse started up again. He put the beam back in the animal's eyes. "It's the light. The idiot's afraid of the dark."

"If you got some duct tape, we can strap that light right where you're holding it," Dwight said.

"No tape."

"I've got some in my truck," Dwight said.

"Well, that's just wonderful." Austin looked at the highway. "You know these batteries are not going to last all night."

"Yeah?"

"One of us is going to have hold this light in this horse's face while the other one drives."

"I'll drive," Dwight said.

"How do you figure that?" Austin asked.

"I wouldn't want you sitting up there taking in that stench."

Austin groaned. "You've got a point. But I can't hang on outside this trailer for sixty miles."

"Nope," Dwight said.

"I'll have to get inside with the horse."

"Yep."

"You know when we get home, if we get home, I'm going to have to kill you. Or something close to it."

"I know."

Dwight held the light while Austin got into the trailer with the stallion. "Easy, boy," he said, touching the horse's side to let him know he was there. "Atta boy." He got to the front and was standing right next to the giant head. "Okay, hand me the light through the slat."

Dwight pushed the flashlight through and it dropped for a second and the horse immediately reacted, but Austin managed the beam back into his face quickly.

"You okay?" Dwight asked.

"Hell, no," Austin said. "Let's go. Don't drive fast, but don't poke around neither."

"All right."

Austin talked to the horse while he held the light, stroked his nose. He heard Myron yell something from the bed of the pickup. He wondered if Dwight would be able to find his way home. He wondered if the cops would pull them over. He wondered if the batteries would last.

# Epigenesis

◆

There is the straightening of line across the riffle, the flash of side in the sleepy pool below the fast water and then the swimming down, tugging, snapping, right-angling turns against the leader and yellow line and then the line is slack. The sun of midmorning bounces its light off the broken surface of the creek while Alan Turing curses and cranks his reel, waiting to see if the Letort's cricket he tied this morning is lost. But on the end of the leader is the cricket and with it is an enormous trout, much larger than the stream should accommodate, much larger than any trout should be, Turing thinks, swallowing hard, much larger than the tug it had less than a minute ago applied against the graphite rod, light pink above its whitish side-floating, all but pushing the leader toward Turing's neoprened legs. The trout is easily three and a half feet long, but no trout is that long, its mouth working about the fly. A steelhead? It can't be in this creek. Turing's muscles quiver with fear and confusion as he once again observes the width and depth of the water, looking upstream and down for another human who might react to the sight and confirm his footing in reality, but there is no one. The fish is at his feet, more of it exposed to air than to water, the opercula covering the gills flowing rhythmically, almost comfortably, thinks Turing, and like lightning striking, the fish says a word, yes, a word. Turing shakes his head, wants to cry, his hands trembling, dropping his rod while his heart stalls, he hears clearly a word, its syllables, it must be a word and the word is **epigenesis**. A closer approach surprises Turing for the bravery it takes, but yields to him no more understanding and no more words, nor the same word from the animal, which is beginning to huff away its life. He touches the head of the trout to feel the smooth slime that encases it, removes the hook that is so insignificant from its lip, and he wonders how he caught the fish, realizes that the fish wanted to be captured, recalling that the trout swam toward him. Turing pushes the animal back toward the pool, the word still in his head, the weight of the fish hanging up against the rocks. Turing sweats and heaves, staring at the glassy eye that, though directed at him, betrays no gaze of its own, and finally backs the fish into the pool and Turing can see just how deep it is, no bottom to find with his staring. The trout sinks and far down Turing can see the kick of its huge tail and believes it still lives. He stands straight in the stream, sucking in a breath of mountain air as he cries and searches the creekside trees for other eyes, human or other, that might be as confused and fearful as his. Turing makes his way free of the stream with the waddle waders make, wondering why its frigid water has not awakened him, wondering if sane men dream such things, cursing his mind for breaking and spilling nonsense about his cranial floor, but on the bank he sits and knows that he is not asleep, not dreaming, believes he is not hallucinating. A light drizzle begins to fall from clouds he has not noticed approaching, his shadow now disappeared in the gray around him. Turing frees himself from his boots and waders, packs them away, slips on his sneakers, and carries his gear through the maples and rhododendrons and the mile back to his car parked at the roadside.

A pickup speeds by on the wet highway, kicking up a spray, but not much of one, while Turing leans against the back of his car. He opens the trunk, tosses in his wader bag, his vest, and his rod, which he has broken down and slipped into its case. He looks down the road and imagines the Swift Camp Creek joining the Red River, imagines the Red River joining the Ohio, and imagines that water on its way to the Mississippi and to the Gulf of Mexico where big fish are supposed to live, but not like that one, not a trout or a steelhead. Giant fish aren't supposed to swim in small water, in holes that should not be, deep and invisible until one is over it; he wonders what would have happened had he stepped into it unknowingly. How many people had? But then it seems stupid to curse the creek when the fish had talked, when the fish had so rudely changed his life.

Turing has put away his gear, hung his waders in the garage, and put his fly boxes on the shelf above his tying table. He sits at his desk, hands together, and waits for his wife to return from Louisville. It's dusk when he hears her car.

Barbara walks past the door of the study, then comes back. "Alan?"

"Yes."

"Why are you sitting here in the dark?" she wants to know.

"No reason, just sitting."

"Are you okay? How was fishing?" Barbara puts her packages down by the doorway.

Turing switches on his desk lamp. The light bothers his eyes. "Fishing was decent, Barbara."

"Catch anything?" She smiles, bends to pick up her things.

"Caught a few." He looks at his desk. "How was Louisville?"

Barbara pauses. "It was fine, Alan."

Later, at dinner, Alan pushes the takeout cartons of Chinese food away and looks at Barbara. "Do you believe that people create their own worlds?" he asks.

"What?" her mouth full.

"Nothing."

"No," she says, wiping her mouth. "Tell me what you're talking about. What worlds?"

"What if, say, an animal, say a dog, talked to you, I mean, spoke a word?"

"Yes?"

"What would you think? Would you think you were crazy? Would you reassess your picture of the world?"

"Hell, no, I wouldn't think I was crazy," Barbara says. "I'd think I was rich. A talking dog, are you kidding? Do you know how much money I could make with a talking dog?" She laughs loudly, reaching for more food. "What's on top of a house? Ruff," she barks.

Turing looks out the window at the dark backyard.

"Did I hurt your feelings?" she asks.

"No."

That night, in the darkness and cold of the room they have shared for twelve years, Barbara halfheartedly leads her husband into lovemaking. He moves with her or for her or because of her, pushing to breach the distance, pushing to make the distance, their orgasms mechanical, standard. Afterward, they lie awake, waiting, just waiting. The light through the window is from the streetlamp, somewhat blue, soft, and lost in the leafless tree limbs just outside.

Turing dreams. He is at a dinner party, across the room his wife is watching him while she talks to a woman in a blue dress and he knows she is talking about him. The food at the party is all the same color and comes by on trays carried by men with no faces. Turing moves through the party looking for someone whose face and name he cannot remember, like a song title, the person is lost in his head and he is becoming anxious. Music comes from somewhere, mechanical and standard, lost in the rhythm of shuffling feet as Turing notices the movement of people in circles, around and around, around the room and around points in space. Turing knows all the faces of the guests and even the faceless waiters. He gets no closer nor farther away from Barbara no matter which way he moves, no matter how fast he moves, and she is talking about him, now to a man in short pants. He takes more

of the colorless food and searches for taste, some texture, anything. The emptiness wakes him with a start,
his heart racing, his breathing short. He thinks about
touching the hand of his wife, but doesn't.

"A fish spoke to me," he tells his wife the next morning,
watching her tie her running shoes, a foot up on the
stool in the kitchen.

"Very nice," she says.

"No, really, a fish said a word to me."

She looks at him.

"I'm not joking, Barbara."

Barbara laughs.

"I'm scared. A fish—a big fish talked to me."

"And what did this fish say?"

"He said 'epigenesis.' I saw its lips move. I heard it."

"Epigenesis," she repeats.

Turing nods.

"And you weren't drinking?"

"No."

"No drugs?"

"Barbara, I'm serious." He pauses, leans back against
the wall by the door. "Never mind."

"Fine," she says, looking at her watch, standing,
looking out the window at the road, "I'll be back in
forty minutes."

He watches her run out of the yard and down the
street. She thought he was joking. He guesses that's
better than her believing him to be crazy.

The rain falls harder while Alan Turing sits behind
the wheel, switching on the wipers to slap away at

the spitting sky, pulling away from the gravel and mud. Turing struggles with remembering his name, recalling lessons from grade school instead, lines of silly poems, word problems of sheep and shingles and there is his name, burned into his mind along with a fish-voice, **"epigenesis."** Goddamn the beast, so big, and why hadn't he brought it home, but instead took pity or obeyed that giant, sad, milk-glass eye?

Alan Turing goes back to the creek, sits on the bank, and looks at the spot where the hole that shouldn't have been there, was. The water is still, un-moving there. He recalls the day JFK was killed, how when the news came over the loudspeaker his second-grade teacher, Miss Young, had put her hands over her ears and run out of the room; he recalls her slip was showing below her navy skirt. He recalls when he awoke during the night on a family car trip and saw the burning cross of a KKK rally and how his father had stepped on the gas to get them away and how they had to load up on food because there was no place for them to stop and eat on the road; the Temptations were playing on the radio. He remembers how Kathy Wilson had let him touch her pubic hair and had kissed his tongue with hers, then told him they had to stop. He remembers how she hadn't told Reggie Davis to stop. So went Reggie Davis's story and Alan Turing, thirteen, believed it.

He tosses a rock into the creek, hoping the trout will show himself. He will not tell this to his wife again. He will not tell anyone that a fish has spoken to him. He will keep it inside his head. He will keep it next to the fact that lately he has not enjoyed sex with his wife. He will keep it next to his fear of escalators. He will keep it next to the fact that he hated the way his uncle hugged him just a little too long.

Another rock breaks the face of the creek and still no trout shows. Turing once had to beat a deer to death with a bat. The animal had been hit by a car and was suffering badly at the side of the road. It was dusk. Alan Turing had no gun. The deer looked at him with big, pathetic eyes and begged for peace. But the animal's life had been stubborn and it took six swings to end it.

The water in the hole begins to roil. And there on the surface of the water, the light through the boughs reflecting off its smooth sides, is the giant trout, floating up as if dead, one glassy eye aimed at Alan Turing. Alan Turing stands and takes a step, water sloshing over his shoe and ankle as he breaks the face of the stream. Another long step and he is just feet from the fish, his breath catching in his chest as he hears the fish say, "I knew you would come back."

"You're real. I thought I had gone mad," Alan Turing says. "My wife thinks I'm crazy."

"You're not happy," the fish says.

Alan Turing shakes his head. "The world has changed. My wife has changed. And I'm afraid I've stayed the same." He looked upstream and then down. "I told her about you this morning and she thought I was joking."

"Take me home with you," the fish says.

"How?"

"Just put me in your car."

So, Alan Turing wraps his arms around the big fish, the slime of its sides staining his shirt, and he hauls it to the bank, pausing and resting there and then starting up the trail. The fish is silent on the trail, its gills heaving just under Alan Turing's chin, the opercula opening and closing, flashing red. At the trailhead, Alan Turing pauses, reconsidering, looking back over his tracks in the direction of the creek and the fish flops in his arms, says, "Put me in the car."

The trout fills the passenger seat. Its head presses against the armrest of the door. Its tail brushes against Alan Turing's thigh. Its eye is pointed toward the roof.

"Tell me about your wife," the trout says.

Alan Turing drives with both hands on the steering wheel, leaning slightly forward. His fingers are stiffening from the work of driving and so he reaches over to turn on the heat.

"What are you doing?" the trout asks.

"I'm turning on the heat."

"Leave it off."

Alan Turing does. "My wife is very smart," he says. He doesn't look at the fish while he speaks. "She's intense and I sometimes wonder what she sees in me." Alan Turing smiles sadly. "Lately, I've been distant and, I guess, not very responsive. I don't know why. Anyway, I became distant and she became distant and the whole thing just kind of snowballed. I've been working a lot lately. But that's not really it. I mean, it hasn't been work. I've been—how can I put it—lost, sick, stupid. I'm simply not happy with life." Alan Turing glances at the trout. The fish looks bored. "I know it sounds dumb. Midlife shit and all that. But now I'm afraid I've pushed Barbara far enough away that she's looking for someone else."

The trout seems to struggle with a breath, flops its tail against the fabric of Alan Turing's trousers.

"We still have sex, but that's all it is, I think. Sex. It feels so empty. It never felt like I had to search for the feeling before. I'm so scared. We don't even argue. We're just creating a gentle, uncrossable distance. And then I get mad and I want to tell her to go away." Alan Turing is crying. "It's life, too, you know. It's this day-to-day stuff. I don't know why I do anything. I do my research, but it's for shit. I read the news and it goes in one eye and out the other. I haven't heard a good joke in years. And my wife is sleeping with someone else and still fucking me."

The fish says nothing.

Alan Turing pulls into his driveway and turns off his car's engine. He gives the trout a look and says, "Wait here." He gets out and walks across the yard, the grass of the lawn he hates so much feeling soft and moist under his feet. His hands are shaking. He enters the house and stands inside the foyer. He calls out for his wife. "Barbara!" There is an urgency in his voice that he hears, that at some other time he might seek to control, but not at this moment. "Barbara!"

Barbara comes down the stairs. She is wearing a robe, a towel wrapped around her head. "What is it?"

"Why do we do this?" Alan Turing asks.

"What's wrong?"

"Everything's wrong, Barbara. Look at us. Look at us."

Barbara clutches her robe closed.

"Yeah, close up. Heaven forbid I should see you naked in the light. It might lead to lovemaking instead of fucking."

"Alan," she complains.

Alan Turing is pacing. He stops and stares at her. "What's happened to us? To everything?" Inside his head, reality seems far away and unreachable. "Come outside with me. I want to show you something."

"I'm not dressed."

"It doesn't matter. Come on. Come on!"

Barbara flinches.

"Come on," Alan Turing says more gently.

"Alan, you're scaring me."

"I'm scared, too."

"What do you want to show me?" she asks.

"Just come with me. Please?"

Barbara nods and steps through the door he is holding open for her. She follows him across the yard. He leads her to his car in the driveway. He turns and watches her look across the street for neighbors.

At the car, he looks in and the big trout is not there. There is a very little minnow dead on the passenger seat of his car. He feels near to fainting and turns, squares his shoulders to Barbara.

"What is it?" she says.

Alan Turing looks at his wife's eyes, tries to hold them, tries to memorize them. He looks at her lips and her ears and her nose. He touches her hair.

"What is it, Alan?"

He says, "I love you."

# The Devolution of Nuclear Associability

◆

We are all too familiar with Saussure's

$$\text{sign} = \frac{\text{Signifier}}{\text{Signified}}$$

and likewise all too familiar with the notion that the *line* separating the signifier and signified is somehow sliding or shifting. And finally, we are as familiar with the instructional icon:

# Arbor

As elementary as these concepts might now seem, I begin with them as Semiotics begins with them.

So, I ask you to imagine a character, *Adam*. Adam is deficient in a singular linguistic way. He is never quite able to say what he means. Adam often gets very close, but never realizes his intention. Adam might attempt to explain the Pythagorean Theorem, but can only manage to get across that the sum of the squares of two sides of a triangle equals the square of the third side, being unable to make clear that the third side is the hypotenuse. Likewise, if Adam means to draw our attention to a right angle, he can only manage *triangle*. So, that space or gap between the signified and the signifier is never quite crossed. We get:

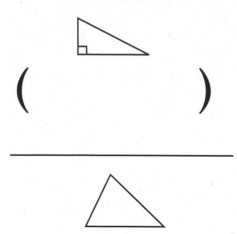

Since nature abhors a vacuum, something must fill that space. To say that it is nothing merely begs the question. For if Adam, with his peculiar problem, were to intend to mean triangle, he would only be able to convey *geometric shape*. We have then:

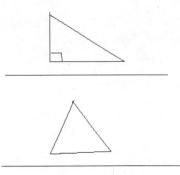

### Geometric shape

If we place above this Adam's attempt to offer the Pythagorean Theorem, then we see a ladder of sorts, which we might consider bounded on either side by some associative thread:

We can well imagine how this disability of Adam's can prove frustrating. Especially when he attempts to, say, summon help to his burning house, he being capable only of directing the firefighters to a house

near his or to one that looks much like his, his meaning becoming twisted in his frantic efforts, much as
our meaning often twists.

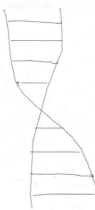

*Meaning* is difficult enough without metaphor
and metonymy. But imagine Adam undertaking to say
something subtle and metaphoric. His meaning will
not only fall short, but might, in fact must, be miscon-
strued by misdirection. His ladder of meaning breaks:

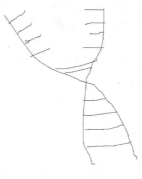

And depending on the situation in which his attempt is made, his broken meaning can accept (un)intentional connotational import, which we'll call *contextual clutter,* and so looks like this:

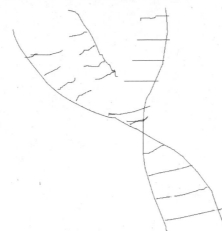

That *new* meaning cannot be denied (whether acquired randomly or designedly), but it was not, in fact, Adam's intention to make that meaning. Too heavy for his initial chain, the new meaning falls off and becomes an attempt at meaning all its own, which might in turn be defended, regretted, or repeated, and certainly twisted.

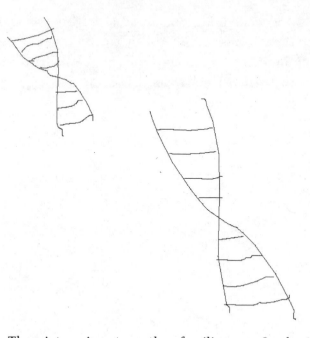

The picture is yet another familiar one. I submit that it is an accurate and even a final representation of meaning. This is the stuff of meaning. Meaning is what we are and we are meaning. Meaning is molecular.

# The Last Heat of Summer

◆

*1 September*

There was nothing outside our town to warn you of its
coming. One second you weren't there and the next
you were. It was more than a post office and more
than a village, but it had no sprawl, it had no outskirts.
The town huddled close together for protection, the
desert everyone loved promising to kill any stray.
There, on spring afternoons and evenings when the
dropping sun washed the sky pink, my friend Errol, a
Kiowa Indian, and I would go out into the countryside
and follow the tracks of coyotes. We saw the animals
frequently and, in the course of watching them, had
discovered several dens in the hills south of town. We
dreamed of finding a lion's den, but never even saw a
lion. The coyotes must have known we were there, staring at them from adjacent ridges through our fathers'
field glasses, but the coyotes never seemed to care, casually letting their pups out to play in the cool air.

Early one evening Errol and I were sitting behind
a boulder and watching two coyotes at the waterhole.
The clouds that had formed above the mountains

to the east never came closer and we could see that it was raining over there. Another coyote appeared suddenly, strolled close and then attacked the male, biting at its hind legs and drawing blood immediately. The wounded animal yelped but didn't retreat, the crimson soaking through his fur. Our eyes were pressed hard against the rubber cups of our glasses' eyepieces.

"Did you see that?" I asked Errol. I could tell by the way he didn't answer that he had.

The animals launched into each other again and if not for the stream of blood from the one's leg we would have been unable to tell them apart. While they tore at each other, the third coyote remained uninvolved and actually seemed to enjoy her drink from the hole. Bites yielded yelps and even though we were some seventy yards away we could hear the growling and snarling. Then one animal lay motionless, the one with the bloody hip. I could see its chest heaving with difficult breaths. The attacking coyote trotted off and soon the female followed.

"Is he dying?" Errol asked.

"I don't know."

"What should we do?"

"What can we do?" We studied for another minute or so. "Let's get closer." I looked at Errol and saw that he was unsure. "Not too close, just closer."

In order to get closer, however, we had to climb down a steep slope covered with loose pebbles and for a second the waterhole was out of our view. When we could see it again the injured animal was gone.

"I want to see the spot where he was on the ground,"
I said.

"Why?"

"I want to see if he left any blood."

"That's crazy." Errol stuffed his binoculars back into
the case, being sure to apply the lens covers. "What's
the big deal about coyote blood?"

"I just want to see it, that's all."

So we walked through the prickly pears and purs-
lane to the waterhole and there it was, on the sand by
the water and some of it on a bleached piece of wood,
the blood of the coyote. It was everything I hoped it
would be, real.


*1 September*

Errol and I spent most of the afternoon packing the
gear for the camping trip we would be taking with
our fathers into the mountains north of Taos. It was
not even fall yet, but there had already been snow up
in Wyoming and Colorado and so we knew that the
nights could be very cold. I was eager to try out the
new sleeping bag my father had bought me. I pulled
the blue bag out of its teal vinyl sack and let Errol feel
the thickness of the fiberfill. He said something about
maybe it being too heavy and it crossed my mind that
he might be jealous. "I don't know," I said, "I'm getting
pretty big now. I think I can manage it." It was an un-
intentional comment on his size; I knew that it bothered him that I had shot up a couple of inches over
the summer while he had remained the same height.

I felt immediately guilty for having said it and I tried to gloss over it by saying, "You might be right though. Some of the trails are mighty steep."

"Yeah, well, I can take the cold," he said.

We cleaned off the campstove and closed it, rolled the bottles of white gas up in a couple of thick towels.

"My father says he's sure we'll see a lion this year," Errol said.

"A lion?" The idea excited me.

"He said there is much talk of a cat around Questa. He said it killed a bunch of sheep and a dog, I think."

I whistled out a breath.

"My father said if we find some sign we'll track it and then we can see it."

"That would be something," I said, even though his talking was sounding like bragging, but I was more interested in the cat. I genuinely hoped his father could track the thing.

"Kiowa are great trackers," Errol said.

"I know."

## 1 September

After Errol went home that night I sat in the den where my mother and father were playing gin. They sat on the sofa and used the coffee table for the cards and I sat on the floor in front of the televsion and watched some kind of spy movie. My mother was wearing a yellow dress with red flowers on it and her hair was pulled back to show her round face and its delicate features, her full lips painted red against her brown skin. Looking at her made me happy and I felt warm, being full of the roast beef dinner we'd just had. My mother laughed a lot and it sounded as if she was winning and my father pretended to be bothered by it all, but I could tell he wasn't. In the movie a man was chasing his double, a man who looked just like him except that he had a scar on his chest. They were on a train and the bad guy kept making everyone think he was the good guy and doing and saying rotten stuff so that they all came to hate the good guy. My mother told my father that she was going to miss us while we were up in the mountains and said she wanted us to be careful. My father and I told her we would be and when I turned back to the television, the train had wrecked and I didn't know which spy was the good one.

*1 September*

My mother was a stalwart believer that breakfast was the most important meal of the day, and especially today, as we were setting out for the wilderness, she fed us well. We had oatmeal and eggs and pancakes with fresh berries. My father read the newspaper and whistled out a breath, said something about the government that neither I nor my mother heard and then put down the paper.

"So, we should be back early on Thursday," he said and then shoveled in a spoonful of oatmeal.

My mother looked at me. "You be sure to change your underwear. I know how you boys get out there. And brush your teeth."

"Yes, ma'am."

The sun was pouring in through the window over the sink and the zinnias my mother had cut and brought in from the garden were glowing. My father was wearing his favorite flannel shirt and I had on one very much like it. We tried to eat everything to please my mother.

We finished breakfast and loaded our gear into the Jeep Wagoneer, making sure to leave plenty of room for Errol and his father's stuff. I petted the head of Lassie, our collie, and then we waved good-bye to my mother as we backed off the driveway and rolled away down our lane, past the gardens and picket fences and past the car-chasing terrier that lived on the corner and often slept in the middle of the street.

## 1 September

The drive north and up into the mountains was beautiful. Errol and I were sitting in the backseat while our fathers talked in the front. Errol's father, whose name was Andy, called my father by his shortened nickname, Oz.

"So, what do you think, Oz?" the Kiowa man said. "Do you think this stuff down in Cuba is a real problem?"

My father shrugged. "I just wish the white people could blow each other up without taking the rest of us with them."

The two men laughed, but Errol and I just looked at each other.

"But life is good for us out here, isn't it, Andy?" my father asked.

"Yes, it is."

We drove up away from the squatty junipers and past the firs into a series of meadows and stands of aspen. We decided to stop at the top of a hill that over-looked a clear, twisting creek that had a beaver dam. The two fathers agreed that the fishing would be good there and so we set up camp. It seemed we all sang as we collected wood for the fire, set up tents, and pre-pared the night's dinner of hot dogs and baked beans from a can. I don't remember what songs we sang, only that we sang.

## 1 September

We sat around the fire after our meal and Errol's fa-ther told us how his people used to come down and raid the Taos Indians, how some of the warriors re-mained to take Taos wives, how they set up a camp in Bear Canyon and lived there in the summers and in the winters moved down to stay in the pueblo, even though they were Kiowa, even though the Kiowa made periodic raids on their village.

The moon was full that night and was bright corn-bread yellow. A few coyotes called out to it and Errol and I watched it, our heads sticking out of the tent we were sharing. Our fathers were still up and talking just yards away.

"I wish I was Indian like you," I said to Errol.

"Why?"

"I don't know, really," I said. "I guess I like the way your father talks about this place. Like it's a part of him."

"My grandfather told me I'm a cat dreamer. And it's true, I have these dreams where a cat moves right through me. I can feel it."

I stared at his profile, his eyes still pointed at the sky. I wondered whether I believed him. I wanted to believe him and was jealous at the thought that it was true. "What kind of cat?" I asked.

"A big one, a lion."

I closed my eyes and looked for my own cat.


*1 September*

Fog hung in patches over the pond and meadow. Errol fished the slow-moving creek below the beaver dam and I worked the expanse of flat, still water above it. It was early, the air still frigid. There was no fish-feeding activity on the surface, so I was casting terrestrials, cinnamon ants, hoppers, and elk-hair caddis flies up current to an undercut bank. I was casting into the weeds and dragging the flies into the water with a splash, the way my father had taught me. "Ground insects always splash into the water," my father told me. "You don't have to cast far. It's all presentation. Everything is presentation."

A big brown took my hopper and then darted for cover around a stump in the pond. I sloshed through the knee-deep water to keep my line clear. It was a big fish, at least twenty inches. My heart was pounding. My breath was short. I could feel Errol watching me. I began to strip in line.

"Not too fast," Errol called to me.

I heeded his warning and calmed myself. I pulled the trout closer and closer and then I could see his eye staring at me on the surface. I was standing at the bank now. I grabbed the fish, slipped out the hook, and dropped it into my creel. I looked down to see Errol and he was waving to me, gave me the okay sign.

### 1 September

We ate the fish that Errol and I caught for breakfast along with scrambled eggs made by Errol's father. The fish were fried with the heads still on and the meat fell away from the skeletons easily. The heat of the cooking fire warmed the front of my body and a cool wind bit pleasantly into my back.

After breakfast, we went hiking up the mountain. We followed the creek for a couple of miles and then veered away from it, climbing to the top of a ridge. We followed the ridge up into stands of aspen trees. We got a quick glimpse of a yearling elk, and then we found the partially devoured carcass of a fawn. The glassy eyes didn't look real. The body was ripped open and the hind legs were gone. Part of the heart was several feet away.

"Lion," Errol's father said. "Look at the claw marks

and the size of the bite." He pointed to the torn, light brown body, but I really couldn't see what he was talking about. "Body's still warm," he said.

Errol and I looked about anxiously. I was both excited and terrified. I wanted to see the animal, see it close up, out there in the woods.

"You boys stay close," my father said.

We continued on through the forest. It was a cloudy day and so the sun never really had a chance to warm things up. I zipped up my jacket and listened for noises as we walked, trying to separate the forest from the sounds of our footfalls. We made it to the high lake and ate a late lunch of cheese sandwiches. Then we started back down. We didn't see the cat, no further sign of it. I was disappointed. But the image of that fawn's heart stayed with me.

## 1 September

There was a lion up there. I didn't get to see it, but I was next to its kill. I saw the animal's heart from which it had taken a bite. In my mind, the cat was gigantic, but in my calmer moments I realized that it was no bigger than a German shepherd dog. I couldn't get to sleep that first night home after the camping trip. I wanted to dream about the lion and nothing else.

While I was awake, I thought about the fact that school would be starting again very soon. A matter of days. Those last days of summer were always the sweetest. The weather was hot, but not unbearable.

There were occasional afternoon showers. And after the rain, when the desert had sucked up the moisture in less time than it had taken to fall, I would walk with Frannie Dawes.

Frannie Dawes lived across the street with her mother. Her father was in and out of the VA hospital in Albuquerque. Frannie was skinny, with little feet, and she played the flute. She liked insects and so I liked her.

Those last days of summer were sweet. And the circus was coming.

## 1 September

Frannie Dawes and I left my house with a sack lunch and my father's binoculars. We didn't see any coyotes, but we walked a long time. We walked along the wash and watched a couple of red-tailed hawks circling and looking for prey. We stayed out until the sun was going down, just talking about this and that. I was floating, feeling happy and lost. And I wanted more than anything to kiss Frannie Dawes, to kiss her on the lips.

We were facing the sunset as we approached the edge of town. There was a broken band of clouds, which the sun had turned golden. Frannie said for me to stop walking and just look at that. "Just look at that," she said. I did and my hand found hers. I had never been so scared in my life. I looked over at her face. She was staring at the horizon at first, but then she looked at me. I don't know how it happened, but somehow I kissed Frannie Dawes. It was a quick kiss, our lips barely touching, but it felt like a gift. Then we walked on, my heart racing around my chest.

### 1 September

The cave was located south of town. Errol, Frannie, and I were there at about dusk. We waited, watching the opening from about fifty yards away. A bat flew out and into the pink sky. Then another and then a swarm. A cloud of bats, their wings grabbing the air and pushing it behind them, sounding together to make a huge scream in the night. Buzzing. My mouth was open at the sight and when I realized it, I shut it. I glanced over at Frannie. Her eyes were so beautiful and full of wonder and I wondered if I could ever look that beautiful to someone. Errol was standing slightly in front of us. He couldn't keep still. He bounced on the balls of his feet. He was so excited by the sight. He said, "Look at that! Would you look at that?!" Then he turned to look at us. Frannie had reached over and taken my hand. Errol saw our fingers tangled together. He gave my eyes a quick brush with his and then turned back to the bats.

"Bats can't see," Errol said. "They're blind and they have sonar, just like navy ships. Some people are afraid of them, but they won't hurt you."

"They give me the creeps," Frannie said, and she held my hand a little tighter.

"That's because you're a girl," Errol snapped.

"They give me the creeps, too," I said.

"Like I said." Errol sighed out a breath. "Come on, let's go back to town."

## 1 September

The circus came. It came into our little town as a parade, music blaring from a marching band, and elephants stomping the streets, leaving them wet with dung and the smell of the circus. We watched the clowns tumble by. We watched the ladies in the skimpy clothes ride by on horseback and we nudged each other with our elbows. We watched the man in the top hat point to us and beckon us to come. Trucks carrying the large cages with the lions and tigers rolled by us. We watched them all the way through town and out to the western edge where they set up camp. Their big tents were beautiful with the sun sinking down behind them. The sounds of the animals rode the wind into the town that night and I went to sleep listening through my open window.

Errol and I sat forward in the bleachers, away from our parents, at the show. Frannie sat with her mother, father, and little brother. We ate popcorn while we waited for the show to start.

"What is it with you and Frannie?" Errol asked.

"What do you mean?"

"I saw you holding her hand."

I was embarrassed. "So?"

Errol looked back at the empty center ring. "I just saw you, that's all."

Then the lights went down and a spotlight came down on the ringmaster. We edged forward on our seats. He lifted his hat to us and introduced the acts and we laughed when the clowns fell and slapped each other and we gasped when the acrobats rolled through the air to be caught in the nick of time by another. And then the lion tamer came out. He was a great big man and he cracked his whip loudly. But it was the cats that captured me and I saw the same thing on Errol's face when I glanced over at him. There were two African lions and a tiger. The tiger was gigantic, much larger than I would have imagined. If the lions had been without manes, then the tiger would have dwarfed them.

The tamer walked confidently around the inside of the big cage. He was wearing a rhinestone-studded vest and so the huge muscles of his arms were plain for all of us to see. He cracked his whip once, twice, three times, and the cats, after a brief complaint, all climbed up on their stools. The tamer shouted unintelligible commands at them with his booming voice. The low growls of the lions clawed into the crowd and I could feel the power, but the tiger was silent. When the audience was oohing and aahing over the tamer placing his head into a lion's mouth, I looked over at the tiger and found the animal staring at me. Amber eyes fixed on me. Unmoving.

*1 September*

The tiger's eyes burned there. A glance at Errol let me know that he was not seeing what I was seeing.

Looking at the tiger caused everything else to disappear. The tamer seemed to do all of his tricks with the lions and left the tiger to stare at me. Then the big man approached the tiger and popped his whip. The report made me jump, but the tiger didn't move a muscle. The tamer snapped the leather cord again and still there was no acknowledgment from the striped cat. The tamer looked to where the cat was looking and he saw me. He looked angry and he said something to the tiger. I couldn't hear his words, only the quality of his sounds, but whatever it was he said, he got the tiger's attention. The tiger looked at him and before anyone knew what had happened, the tamer was on the ground in a pool of blood. The big iron gate swung open by itself and the big tiger stepped out of the cage. People screamed and ran, some down to the aisles and out, pushing and trampling, and others scurried up to the top of the bleachers, packing in together with nowhere to go. I don't know which way Errol ran, but I stayed put, right there in the front row. No one was near me. I watched the tiger rip open the arm of a circus roadie who was trying to toss a net over him. Another roadie was reluctantly trying to draw a bead on the cat with a rifle. The screaming and shouting fused into a kind of meaningless roar. Then the cat was standing in front of me. I heard my mother's voice pierce the deadened hush. The tiger turned his enormous head and took my body into his mouth, closed his jaws about my waist. But he didn't bite down, though I could feel the coolness of several of his teeth against the skin of my back and sides.

## 1 September

The tiger carried me in his mouth down the aisle toward the exit. I looked up and saw my mother in the
crowd on the bleachers, her face frozen in a scream,
but I couldn't hear any sound coming out of her. I
could hear only the raspy breathing of the big cat. I
saw my father trying to push and weave through the
pulsing tangle of bodies. People scurried for cover on
tops of trucks and cars and behind refuse barrels and
small boulders as we passed. I could feel the pad of
each footfall against the stiff ground. Errol was standing in the bed of a pickup with his father and I could
see that he wanted to run to my rescue, but was being
held back. Then, in his face, I could see that Errol did
not want to save my life, but that he wanted to sever
my connection to the cat. He was not concerned
about my welfare. He was jealous. I stared at his eyes
as the tiger carried me past him. I smiled.

But where was the animal taking me? I began to
grow fearful. I found it remarkable that this was my
first pang of concern for myself. I was just coming to
realize that the cat had captured me, that it was not
the other way around. The tiger carried me off into
the night, toward the big wash.

## 1 September

As I was being carried between the teeth, I tried to
remember everything I knew about tigers. I didn't
know much. I knew that tigers had poor vision. I knew
that they had a weak sense of smell. I knew that they

hunted by sound. I knew that they were aggressive hunters. I knew they were sometimes man-eaters. The cat put me down near some large rocks and walked away a few steps, then dropped to the ground, seemingly exhausted. I was too afraid to stand or even sit up. I moved my foot barely an inch, my toes moving a pebble on the ground not quite enough to push it from its spot in the sand, and the tiger let out a warning rasp of breath, a sound that was not quite a roar, but substantially more than a purr. So, I lay as still as possible, trying to slow my breathing and calm my heart. I wondered how long it would be before my father came for me. I wondered if some man from the circus was at that moment drawing a bead on the cat with a scoped rifle loaded with a dart. I kept seeing Errol's face.

*1 September*

The tiger and I slept and morning came. I had been cold all night, but for some reason I was able to sleep through until light. The tiger got up and paced a circle around me. Then I heard the voice of the circus master of ceremonies. He was calling my name and I could tell he was drawing nearer. He got closer and closer and the tiger heard him, too. I called out to him and told him to stay away. But he came anyway. The tiger roared, his big noise echoing off the rocks, but he came anyway. The big cat hissed at him when he was in sight, but the master of ceremonies came anyway. He was just yards from me, reaching out to me, calling me by my full name, telling me he was going to take me to my parents. Then the tiger ran at him. The tiger bit into his stomach and he screamed out some name I didn't know. I cried out into the morning air. The tiger clawed at his face, erased it. The tiger glanced at me, then lapped at the man's life, licked up the red juice of his existence.

## 1 September

The tiger and I slept again until the sun was straight overhead and the heat was considerable. The tiger got up and paced circles around me once more. Then I heard the voice of Errol. He was calling my name and I could tell he was drawing nearer. He got closer and closer and the tiger heard him, too. I called out to him and told him to stay away. But he came anyway. The tiger roared, his big noise echoing off the rocks, but he came anyway. The big cat hissed at him when he was in sight, but my best friend came anyway. He was just yards from me, reaching out to me, telling me that I was his best friend and that he would save me. Then the tiger ran at him. The tiger bit into his stomach and he screamed out Frannie's name. I cried out into the afternoon air. The tiger clawed at his face, erased it. The tiger glanced at me, then lapped at Errol's life, licked up the red juice of his existence.

## 1 September

It was late summer, just days before school would start. That perfect time. The heat was just so.

The tiger and I slept again until the sun was starting down in the west. I could feel the air beginning to cool just a little. The tiger got up and paced circles around me once more. I had grown accustomed to it. Then I heard the voice of my mother. She was calling my name and I could tell she was drawing nearer. She got closer and closer and the tiger heard her, too. I called out to her and told her to stay away. But she came anyway, saying that I was a baby and that she loved me. The tiger roared, his big noise echoing off the rocks, but she came anyway. The big cat hissed at her when she was in sight, but my mother came anyway. She was just yards from me, reaching out to me, telling me that I was her reason for living. Then the tiger ran at her. The tiger bit into her stomach and she screamed out my father's name. I cried out into the evening air. The tiger clawed at her face, erased it. The tiger glanced at me, then lapped at my mother's life, licked up the red juice of her existence.

## 1 September

The night sky was lavender in the west and a deep purple in the east. It was late summer, just days before school would start. My mother's body parts lay with those of Errol and the master of ceremonies.

The tiger and I had been sleeping again, our bodies touching. The air was stiffly cold and there was a persistent wind. The tiger got up, but did not pace this time, instead he sat beside me, sniffing the breeze. Then I heard the voice of my father. He was calling my name and I could tell he was drawing nearer. He got closer and closer and the tiger heard him, too. I called out to him and told him to stay away, told him what had happened to Mother. But he came anyway, saying that I was his son and that he would protect me. The tiger roared, his big noise echoing off the rocks, but he came anyway. The big cat hissed at him when he was in sight, but my father came anyway. He was just yards from me, reaching out to me, telling me that he would save me. Then the tiger ran at him. The tiger bit into his stomach and he screamed out my name. I cried out into the night. The tiger clawed at his face, erased it. The tiger glanced at me, then lapped at my father's life, licked up the red juice of his existence.

## 1 September

The tiger was asleep. It was late summer, just days before school would start and it was snowing in the desert. I walked a circle around the sleeping beast, kicking through the bones and flesh of my life, the parts of my friend and my mother and my father and of someone I did not know, but who had come to try to save me. The blood of my father stuck to the sole of my shoe and made a kissing sound. I stepped on my mother's delicate fingers.

# Randall Randall

◆

RANDALL HALPERN RANDALL

189 Wayland Avenue, Apt.51
Providence, Rhode Island

*8:10 a.m., Sunday, November 23, 1980*

Miss Holly Diehl
Apt.41
189 Wayland Avenue
Providence, RI

Dear Holly:

I am distressed that it has come to this. I had hoped that there would be no reason for me to compose this letter, but it seems the matter at hand will not straighten itself out, considering this morning's condition in the driveway rear of this building.

*Please permit me to state MY SIDE of the matter in question!!!*

My dear wife, a good woman who knits constantly and who makes baby booties for people she doesn't even

know, has enjoyed over 20 years of extremely peaceful and harmonious relations with the tenants in this
building, and *I* certainly have tried my best to pre-
serve such a condition in spite of some recent goings-
on, such as door slamming by tenants on the fourth
and sixth floors, etc.

We have attempted to quietly and without disturbing
anyone else, on any floor, take care of the rubbish
and/or garbage from our apartment . . . to the large
green Dumpster, as detailed in our lease and yours . . .
daily (not just weekends as you seem to have deduced
per Claudia!). *However, I usually do it . . . and a major
reason is that Claudia suffered a fracture to her kneecap
(patella) some time back when she fell on some ice outside
the convenience store and had to wear a brace for weeks.
And of course I have thrombophlebitis, as did our late presi-
dent Mr. Nixon, two years ago throughout my left leg and
must watch myself when descending the 87 steps down to*
the first floor and out the rear door of this building!!!

I contacted Mr. Harry Bottoms following your "to
whom it may concern" note (which I still have in
my possession) and asked him WHO was probably
the nicest and most quiet and agreeable tenant in the
building—aside from him and Lucy. He said without pause that it is YOU!!! That is WHY I could not
understand HOW *any such fine person* would block
the rear door to prevent passage to the big green
Dumpster . . . . . . *aside from* the probability that the
fire department could NEVER get in in case of a fire
in the building!!! I remember vividly when those yel-

low lines were painted, and I NEVER saw any car in that area right up close blocking the door until your car was there!!!

You KNOW that once I stopped into your fine apartment and was received most cordially, and enjoyed speaking with you about your plants and collection of small dinner bells, etc. I could NOT somehow believe that it was YOUR car (never thought it was for one minute) that was blocking us from the Dumpster.

I was planning to seek you out for a discussion of the matter, but the condition, and it was a condition and not a situation as my wife insists, was so serious this morning that I had to state MY side of the case to Mr. Pluckett!!! I HOPE that this will be the end of it—and that my poor wife won't have to cart our waste out and around, so publicly, around three (3) sides of the building to reach the Dumpster!!! Mr. Bottoms was just up here again—Claudia spoke with him at length only to discover that you and others have accused me of *overreacting*. Please do not speak about me further and I shall do the same for you.

Sincerely,

R.H.R

P.S.—I don't care what you or anyone else thinks, I am NOT a "troublemaker" and want a peaceful home just as you no doubt do. I DO try to be alert, however, because there have been several burglaries in the 27 years Claudia has been here and the 16 years that I have been here. And of course the Osco drugstore was broken into again last week.


Randall folded the letter and sealed it in an envelope. He waved it in the air in front of his wife's face as if to say, "This should take care of it."

"It's not such a big deal, Randall," Claudia said.

"What if I were breaking the rule?" Randall asked. "What if it was me? You think it would just be let go? No, it wouldn't." He sat down at the kitchen table and scratched at a chip in the Formica. "No, it wouldn't and I'll tell you why. It's because she's a young woman and Pluckett's a dirty old man."

Claudia slapped a skillet onto a burner of the gas stove. She laughed.

"Shut up."

"I bet old Pluckett is down there right now having a little party with Miss Diehl." She melted butter in the pan while she opened the refrigerator.

"I only want one egg this morning," Randall said.

"Bacon or sausage?"

"Sausage."

"We're out of sausage," Claudia said.

"Then why did you ask me?"

She put the bacon on the counter next to the carton of eggs. "I wanted to give you a choice."

"But I didn't have a choice."

"You chose, didn't you? You just made the wrong choice." She cracked an egg into the hot skillet. It sizzled.

"Well, I don't want bacon," Randall said.

"Then I won't make you any."

He looked at her in her lavender robe and cream-colored slippers. She was dressed in street clothes, but still she wore that robe over them and those slippers. He hated the way the heels of her feet looked, hard and callused, white, porous.

"Do you want toast?"

"Is there any bread?"

"Yes."

"Then, yes, I want toast."

Claudia flipped one of the eggs. "I broke your yolk," she told him. She lit a cigarette and put the lighter back down on the sill above the sink.

"I want to put plastic runners down over the carpet in the front room," Claudia said.

"Plastic runners?"

"To protect the carpet from wear."

Randall laughed. "Wear? Oh, yeah, from all the visitors we get."

Claudia fell silent as she slid the eggs onto the plates. She pulled the bread from the toaster and put breakfast in front of Randall. She sat with him at the table.

Randall buttered his toast. "This neighborhood is going to hell."

Claudia tore her toast and dipped a corner of it into the yolk of her egg.

"Gangs and drugs," Randall said. "Punks." He watched Claudia eat for a while. "What's wrong with you?"

"Nothing's wrong with me."

"Something's wrong," he said.

"I'll tell you what's wrong. I don't have anybody to talk to. That's what's wrong."

"Here we go again," Randall sighed it out. "I'm talking to you right now."

Claudia continued to eat.

Randall put his fork down. "Listen, I'm going out to get my medicine. Is there any money in the house?"

Claudia looked up at him. "In my purse."

"What?"

"There's some money in my purse," she repeated.

Randall went into the front room and grabbed Claudia's pocketbook from the buffet. He brought it back to the doorway of the kitchen and found the money in it. "Do you need anything while I'm out?"

"No."

"I'm not going out again, so tell me now if you need anything."

"I don't need anything."

"Okay, but I asked. You can't tell me I didn't ask."

Randall walked out, pulling the door closed behind him. He went down one flight of stairs and stood at number 41. He slipped the note under the door of Holly Diehl's apartment. At that moment the door opened and there was Holly Diehl, a small woman with short blond hair and she was looking at Randall.

"Just delivering a note to you," Randall said.

Holly Diehl bent and picked it up, looked at the envelope.

Randall realized that he had not put her name on it.

"How do you know it's for me?" she asked.

"It's for you," he said and he turned away and started walking toward the stairs.

"Is this from you?" Holly Diehl asked.

But Randall was gone. He walked down the stairs and out onto Wayland Avenue. The cold wind blew open his jacket and he pulled it closed, zipped it as he walked. He looked in through the window of the Oriental rug store where none of the salesmen spoke English, at least pretended not to speak English. Randall had gone in when the shop first opened, but when he figured out how much they were trying to tell him a rug sold for he got mad. He turned his gaze away when one of the mustached salesmen waved to him.

A blast of heat pushed through Randall when he entered the Osco drugstore and made him too hot. He unzipped his jacket and let out a breath.

"Morning, Mr. Randall," the young clerk, Susie, said. She was setting up a display of blank videotapes.

"Hi, Susie," Randall said. He liked her, liked to look at the way her makeup curved up at the corners of her eyes. He had always thought that Claudia would look good like that, but had never said anything, knew she would take it the wrong way. Claudia could try something, he thought, more makeup or wear her hair differently. She didn't even try. All she ever did was complain about her knee. Susie always smiled at him, so he knew he was still an attractive man.

At the back of the store, the druggist, a fat man named Willy, was in his booth. Randall hated looking up at the man. He didn't like Willy, was sure that the man was cheating him somehow, maybe putting less medicine in each capsule.

"How's the pressure?" Willy asked.

"Under control," Randall said. "How's yours?"

"Oh, I don't have a problem. I watch my diet and walk to work."

Randall nodded as Willy turned away to collect his medicine. "Sure you do, you fat bastard," he said under his breath.

"Excuse me?" Willy said.

"Nothing."

"Oh, I thought you said something." Willy reached through the window and handed down the vial of pills in a small white bag. "There you go."

"Thanks."

"You ought to get some exercise," Willy said. "Gotta stay in shape just to run from the thugs in this neighborhood nowadays."

"You can't outrun them bastards," Randall chuckled.

"Don't need to. Not now."

Randall nodded and walked away down the aisle of foot-care items. He remembered once when he had athlete's foot and how good that spray had felt. It was funny he had thought then, and thought now, that his feet didn't usually feel good, bad, or otherwise. It was something when that spray had felt good. He met Susie at the checkout.

"Is that it?" Susie asked.

"That's it." Randall looked at her eyes. "I like your eyes," he said. "The way you paint them." He had never mentioned them to her before. "How's school?"

"Stopped going."

"Oh. Are you still going out with that guy? That cook guy?" Randall remembered his white clothes from when he would pick up Susie from the drugstore.

"No. He thought he was hot stuff because he was going to Johnson and Wales."

"Oh."

"I'm trying to get a job as a cosmetician," Susie said.

"You'll be good at it. You always look really pretty." He paused, watching her nails on the register keys. "I hope you don't mind me saying that."

"No, I don't. Thank you, Mr. Randall. That will be twelve forty-seven."

He handed her a ten and a five. "This stuff just keeps going up."

"Everything does," Susie said. She counted his change out to him. "Want your receipt?"

"I guess."

"Bye now."

Randall waved and walked away, the blast of heat at the doorway bothering him once more as he exited.

Randall paused at the entrance to his building, looked up its side to his window. He decided to walk around back and check on the situation with the driveway and the Dumpster. He rounded the corner and saw the car before he was there. He couldn't believe it. After all his complaining and his last letter, here was Holly Diehl's car, big as life, in the very same spot, blocking the Dumpster. He saw exhaust coming out of the tailpipe and realized that the car was running. Holly Diehl must have just run inside for something. He walked to the driver's side and peered through the window at the purse on the seat. Dumb girl, Randall thought.

Mr. McRae came out of the back door with a bag of garbage and had to squeeze by the blue Honda.

"Can you believe this?" Randall said.

McRae looked at the car. "Pretty tight."

"I've begged her not to park here. It's a fire zone, you know."

McRae nodded and tossed his bag into the container. "I guess it's not a good idea, all right." He was back at the door now. "Nice car, though." He was gone.

Randall looked at the car, then at the closed door. He thought about taking Holly Diehl's purse, to teach her a lesson, then it occurred to him that he should just take her car. He could get into her car and park it around the block. She'd get the point then.

There was no one on the street at that moment and Randall opened the car door. His heart was racing. He looked around again, then fell in behind the wheel, keeping his eye on the door of the building. He stepped on the clutch, put the car into reverse, and released the brake. He backed out slowly, still watching for Holly Diehl. He drove forward away from Wayland Avenue and toward the stop sign at the corner, but he didn't stop, he rolled through it, turning right and noticing behind him a Providence city police car. The cop turned on his blue light.

Randall was sitting in Holly Diehl's car, her open pocketbook beside him. He had taken the car without her permission. He had stolen it. His foot pressed more firmly on the accelerator. The policeman honked his horn. Randall looked at him in the mirror, saw the cop see him looking. He floored it. The car lurched forward and Randall sped away toward the university. The cop turned with him and switched on his siren. Randall felt a pressure in his chest. He careened through a series of alleys and side streets and lost the police car when it slid into a white Plymouth. He saw a cop talking on his radio as he rolled out of sight.

Randall was terrified. He was a criminal on the run. Holly Diehl had no doubt called the police by now to report her car stolen. It occurred to Randall that the policeman could have gotten hurt in the crash. What if that had happened? He would be to blame. He saw the man on the radio, but what if he was calling for an ambulance? What if he had sustained internal injuries or had a bad heart? He could be dying. Randall Halpern Randall could be a murderer. He looked at the little white bag on the seat beside him. He needed one of the pills now. He tried to breathe calmly and deeply, tried to slow his body down. What he needed to do was stop the car and get out, run, hide, and sneak back to his apartment. No one knew that he was the car thief. McRae had seen him by the car though. He needed to get to a phone and call Claudia, tell her to tell anyone who asked for him that he was in the bathroom or something like that. He began to slow to a stop when another siren blast pushed his foot to the floor. The tires of the blue Honda squealed as he narrowly missed hitting a woman with a sheepdog. A light snow began to fall. The cop was right behind him, talking on his radio as he drove. Randall found himself on busy Thayer Street, college students everywhere, cars everywhere, people pointing.

There were two police cars behind him now, lights flashing, sirens blowing. Randall imagined he heard his name over a loudspeaker. He made a sharp right and headed down the bus-only tunnel toward downtown. The police were caught off guard by this maneuver and slammed into each other at the mouth of the tunnel.

To Randall's surprise there were no police at the bottom of the tunnel. He screeched to a halt and got out of the car, ran along Main Street for a half block, then up through someone's yard, through a couple of yards and up the hill until he was on the campus. In fact, he was suddenly back on Thayer Street, just a block from the accident involving the two police cars. People were standing around, watching, telling each other what they had seen. But no one was looking at Randall even though he was panting and his clothes were grass- and dirt-stained from his scurry up the hill. He walked away from the commotion, looking up at the snow, which was falling harder now. The white flakes made him think of his white bag and he remembered that he had left his medicine sitting on the seat of Holly Diehl's car.

He found a phone booth on a corner in front of a gas station. He closed the door, fumbled through the change in his pocket, dropped in a quarter and called Claudia.

"Where are you?" Claudia asked.

"Shut up and listen," he barked.

"Don't you tell me to shut up," she said. "Where are you?"

"Has anyone asked for me?"

"Randall? What's going on?"

"Has anyone asked for me?" he repeated.

"No, no one has asked for you. Why?" He could hear her sitting down on the recliner. "Where are you?"

"If anyone calls or comes by, just tell them I'm in the bathroom."

"Why?"

"Just do it!"

"Don't yell at me," Claudia said.

"I'm sorry. Do it, please?" Randall hung up the phone, knowing that she wouldn't do it. An ambulance rolled by him, lights flashing. The cop was hurt. He knew it. He couldn't count on Claudia. He was suddenly very cold. The snow was beginning to stick to the grass and bushes.

Randall pushed through the wind to the gas-station office. He pieced together forty cents and dropped the coins into the vending machine. He collected his bag of cheese curls from the tray and pulled it open, began to eat as he watched the weather. The man behind the desk, a big greasy man was staring at Randall. Randall left, shoving the remains of his snack into the pocket of his jacket.

Randall counted his money. He had nearly seven dollars, not enough for anything, certainly not enough for a life on the lam. If only that cop hadn't died in that collision. He was sure the matter could be straightened out if not for that. The cold air was beginning to make his lungs ache when he entered a branch of his bank that he had never visited. There was no line and he went directly to a teller, a youngish woman with big glasses and a gold crown that showed in the back of her mouth when she said, "May I help you?"

"I'd like to withdraw some money," Randall said. He felt his pocket and realized he didn't have his checkbook. "But I'm afraid I don't have my checkbook."

"What's your account number then?" the woman asked.

"I don't know."

She looked at him over the rim of her glasses.

"My name is Randall, Randall Randall," he said.

"Randall Randall," she repeated. "Would you mind waiting here for a second?"

"I just want my money," Randall said.

"I'll be right back." The woman fell away from her stool and walked briskly across the floor to another woman and together they regarded Randall.

Randall looked around. The bank was empty of customers. The guard was by the door looking at him. He looked up and saw the video camera looking at him. Randall began to whistle. He turned, continuing to whistle as he moved toward the door.

"Sir," the young teller called to him, but Randall was gone. He ran down the street and around the corner, stopping finally, hands on knees, panting.

Randall went back to Thayer Street and boarded

a bus. There were a couple of kids in the back and a blind man up front next to the driver. They rolled toward the tunnel and Randall saw the faces of the policemen. Their cars were connected to purple tow trucks with *Buzz* painted on the doors. The bus passed by and went through the tunnel. Randall looked at his watch and thought about that armed-forces ad that said soldiers did more before eight than most people did all day. It was nine-thirty.

Randall wandered into a McDonald's to get warm. He bought a cup of coffee and sat in the middle of the restaurant, away from the windows. His mind was racing, but could find nowhere to go. He wouldn't be able to sit here forever. Too long and the workers would get suspicious. Besides, the little, yellow, plastic chairs hurt his butt.

A man in a tattered coat had been sitting in a booth when Randall arrived. He wasn't eating or drinking, just sitting. A kid in a McDonald's hat came and asked him to leave.

"It's cold out there," the man said.

"I'm sorry, sir, but you're going to have to leave."

"It's cold out there."

The kid looked back into the kitchen and caught the eye of another man. He said something to someone Randall couldn't see and came out to the scene.

"He won't go," the kid said.

"Sir, we're trying to run a business here," the new man said. He was tall, lanky, and not too old himself. He wore a brass tag that said MANAGER.

"And I'm trying to stay the fuck alive."

"Listen," the manager was getting tough. "You gotta get out of here right now."

"Or what?" The man in the tattered clothes looked the manager up and down. "Or what? You candy-ass, made-up little prick-faced boy scout."

The manager got mad. "Listen, asshole, the police are coming, already been called."

"The police are coming," the man repeated. "Is that because you can't *handle* the situation?" The man pulled himself up and out of the booth.

The manager and the kid fell back a step.

"Boo," the man said.

The manager got mad and started for the man in the tattered clothes, but the kid stopped him.

"You'd better stop him," the man said, headed for the door. "Don't make me have to hurt the sorry-ass."

The manager stopped pushing and said, "Get out of here, you boozed-up, pathetic, homeless mother-fucker."

The man in the tattered clothes stopped, holding the door open and looked back at the manager. His eyes were steady. "I ain't pathetic."

Randall watched the man walk past the window and out to the street. He got up himself and threw away his empty cup. He had to use the toilet, but he wanted to be gone when the police arrived.

Randall Randall was scared. He couldn't go home and he had no one to whom he could turn. He thought about the people who liked him. Susie liked him. He

liked her. Maybe she would help him. He wondered
what she could do, being just a cashier at the Osco.
She could go to his apartment and get the checkbook.
He would call Claudia and tell her that Susie was coming by for it, but then Claudia would see Susie and get
jealous, jealous of her youth, jealous of her makeup,
and then she would get mad and not give it to her.
For that matter, why couldn't Claudia just bring the
checkbook to him herself or even go to the bank and
bring him the cash? Because she wouldn't, that was
why. She had always insinuated that he was only interested in her money and this would just prove it.
And what would he say when she asked him when he
was coming home? It was her fault that he was in this
mess. He had no problem with the Dumpster, he was
just worried about her knee, all her complaining.

Randall went back to his neighborhood and from a
couple of blocks away he could see that things weren't
quite right. There were two cops standing on the side-
walk across the street from his building.

He found another pay phone, this one in the back
of an arcade. This phone had a dial and it felt funny
on his finger; he had to work to remember his number.
It was difficult for him to hear over the bells and buzz-
ers of the nearest pinball machine, but he knew that
Claudia sounded funny when she answered.

"Oh, hello, Randall," Claudia said. "Where are you,
dear? You're late. I've been so worried."

Randall hung up. He looked over to find the leather-
jacketed, late-teens pinballer staring at him. "What are
you looking at?" Randall asked.

"Nothing," the kid said, staring right him. "I'm look-ing at nothing."

Randall got mad for a second, then became afraid. He left the arcade and decided the public library was a good place to hide and keep warm.

The very tall woman with the tower of books in her arms disappeared down the stairs, leaving Randall alone on the floor, he believed. He sat on a step stool in the middle of an aisle, a book full of pictures of India on his lap. He'd never wanted to go to India and these pictures of sand and elephants and cobra snakes and people with spotted foreheads weren't causing him to want to go there now, but still he wished he were there.

He looked through many, many books about Asia, suffering through the occasional visitor to his section of the stacks. Out the window he could see the sky starting to darken, the snow still falling. The library would close soon and he figured it was best to get out without being asked, so he left.

It was nearly five and the Osco would be closing. He wanted to catch Susie as she was leaving work and ask her to help, though he wasn't sure what he would be asking her to do. Perhaps she would allow him to sleep at her place. It was much colder now and the snow was piling up.

Randall was glad it was dark, feeling he could now move about more freely. His jacket was not nearly warm enough. If he had a credit card he could just take off, go to the bus station or the airport, but he didn't have one. A life on the lam didn't sound so bad, city to city, new people.

Susie was bundled up in her long, down parka, coming out of the front door of the drugstore. The coat was a dark pink and seemed to match her eye makeup. Randall was standing at the corner of the building, at the entrance to the alley, in the shadows.

"Susie," he whispered to her, startling her. "Susie, it's me, Randall Randall."

She looked at him, clutching her bag. "Mr. Randall?" Susie did not come closer. "The police came in today asking questions about you."

"I need your help, Susie."

Susie looked up and down the street, took a step away. "Listen, I've got to go."

"I didn't do anything, Susie."

The young woman walked away, looking over her shoulder at Randall. The snow swirled around her.

Randall went back into the alley and fell to sitting on the ground, leaning against the brick wall, between a green Dumpster like the one behind his building and some empty cardboard cartons. He heard the back door of the Osco open and he pushed and pulled himself to his feet, his legs stiff. He saw Willy, the druggist locking up.

"Willy," Randall said.

"Who's there?"

"It's me."

Willy put the package he was holding into his other hand and reached into his pocket.

Randall moved closer. The flash hurt his eyes. He felt a dull push at his middle and he was confused. He was sitting on the ground, looking down at his lap. His ears were ringing. He moved his eyes back up to see Willy. The fat man showed fear. Randall saw something drop from the fat man's hand. Randall rocked in the cold air, then lay back, looked up at the snow.

PERCIVAL EVERETT is Distinguished Professor of English at the University of Southern California. His most recent books include *James*, *Dr. No* (finalist for the NBCC Award for Fiction and winner of the PEN/ Jean Stein Book Award), *The Trees* (finalist for the Booker Prize and the PEN/Faulkner Award for Fiction), *Telephone* (finalist for the Pulitzer Prize), *So Much Blue*, *Erasure*, and *I Am Not Sidney Poitier*. He has received the NBCC Ivan Sandrof Life Achievement Award and the Windham Campbell Prize from Yale University. *American Fiction*, the feature film based on his novel *Erasure*, was released in 2023. He lives in Los Angeles with his wife, the writer Danzy Senna, and their children.

*Damned If I Do* has been typeset in Charlotte,
a typeface designed by Michael Gills.

Book design by Wendy Holdman.
Composition by Stanton Publication Services, Inc.
Manufactured by BookMobile on acid-free paper.